Labeled for Death

Michele Drier

To my June!
Love and hugs
Michele

LABELED FOR DEATH

Copyright © 2013 Michele Drier

All rights reserved. Without limiting the rights under copyright reserved above, no part of this publication may be reproduced, stored in or introduced into a retrieval system, or transmitted, in any form, or by any means (electronic, mechanical, photocopying, recording, or otherwise) without the prior written permission of both the copyright owner and the above publisher of this book.

This is a work of fiction. Names, characters, places, brands, media, and incidents are either the product of the author's imagination or are used fictitiously. The author acknowledges the trademarked status and trademark owners of various products referenced in this work of fiction, which have been used without permission. The publication/use of these trademarks is not authorized, associated with, or sponsored by the trademark owners.

Formatted by IRONHORSE Formatting

ISBN-13: 978-1491043059

BOOKS BY MICHELE DRIER

Amy Hobbes Newspaper Mysteries

Edited for Death
Labeled for Death

The Kandesky Vampire Chronicles

Book One, SNAP: The World Unfolds
Book Two, SNAP: New Talent
Book Three, Plague: A Love Story
Book Four, Danube: A tale of Murder
Book Five, SNAP: Love for Blood
Book Six, SNAP: Happily Ever After? (Coming in Fall 2013)

Dedication

For Bethie
Onward

CHAPTER ONE

This meeting isn't going well.

I make a move to the left and whack my ankle on an open file drawer. It doesn't make my eyes water, but it does wake me up. I hate meetings and this one has sent me into a daydream far away from here.

Clarice rounds my office door, full spate into a sentence. "...but if it's not just a fight...". She's oblivious to the room full of people, who give her the fish eye. I never know if she's talking to me, herself or somebody on the earbud of her cell. This time, she's somewhere in between, talking herself through what she wants to tell me.

"I just don't know how long the body's been there. The autopsy won't finish until tomorrow morning and there's just not enough to rate page one." She looks up and light dawns in her eyes that she's walked into some sort of gathering. "What's going on?"

I'm Amy Hobbes, the managing editor of the Monroe *Press* and Clarice is my best reporter. She can sense a story happening instantly. If it's on her beloved police beat.

"We're discussing the mega-church expansion. What's not page one?" Trust me, the words "page one" from Clarice

1

wake me up.

"They found a body." Clarice says.

She stops talking for several seconds, toying with me like a cat with a field mouse, so I finally cave. "OK, I give. Who's 'they' and where's the body?"

Clarice quivers. I realize she's shaking herself, bringing her brain back from whatever path it's been on. "I'm sorry, I just figured out you guys are in a meeting. 'They' is the county sheriff's department. And 'where' is the Govicche vineyard. The one by the river. Don't let me interfere, I know this isn't page one."

Right, she's not interfering. Not now that she has our attention. Not when she has my attention. And I have to pay attention. As the ME of the *Press*, I'm responsible for the news that gets into the paper. Here in Monroe murder isn't an everyday occurrence, so each one gets scrutiny.

I turn to the five eager faces around my desk, all focused on Clarice. Murder's still a cool topic in the newsroom and this also gets them out of trying to wrangle a coverage plan that Don Roberts, the religion reporter, will do his best to overturn.

I try not to let too much show when I say, "Let's come back to the church discussion later. Come prepared with story ideas and contacts from your beat." The reporters gather up their notes and shuffle out of my office, half relieved the meeting is over and half pissed because Clarice is front-and-center again. I feel a "mom-always-liked-you-best" undercurrent around Clarice, and they may be right.

"Well, you're the only one in town who seems to be able to derail the mega-church discussion," I say to the blond. "So tell."

"I was just doing my rounds when a lot of activity started at the Sheriff's office." Clarice is a rangy blond who loves the cop shop. Particularly after she met Jim Dodson, former Sheriff of San Juan County. And the interest has gotten more acute since Dodson was appointed Sheriff here in Madison

County. This department is larger, better funded and more active. Currently, it's even money whether he'll run in the next election.

"I saw three deputies run out the back and take off code three, so I got my car and followed." She has a small smile. "You'd think they'd figure out it's dead easy to follow them when they're doing lights and sirens."

"And...?" I don't want to rush her, but if her head's still with Jim Dodson, this could run long.

"By the time I got there, they'd taped the scene—that's pretty funny, looking at a bunch of grape vines wound up with yellow tape—and the crime scene guys were right behind me. They wouldn't let me in but a deputy said they'd found a body. I had to wait until the Public Information Officer showed up to get anything." She shakes her head, whether from the stupidity of the cops following procedures or the length of time it took to get her questions answered. Clarice is pretty much a cat person—it's all about her.

"And the PIO said...?" This is like pulling teeth, not her usual vomit of all the facts.

"They'd found a dead guy tucked under the vines in one row. It was hard to see, with the grapes ripe. The bunches and vines are almost trailing on the ground. The *jefe* of a harvesting crew spotted the body as he was marking rows to cut,"

Her use of the Spanish *jefe* for boss alerted me. "Was the guy a worker?"

"Oh, yeah. The tentative ID from another worker is that the dead guy was an illegal, hired on for the harvest."

"A tentative ID? That was fast."

She nods. "Some of these crews stick together. They've worked together for years, following harvests, then back to Michoacán for a few months with their families. So I think— the PIO won't confirm—that the *jefe* was the one who ID'd the vic."

If I don't stop her, Clarice will drop into cop-speak faster than a code three high-speed chase on the freeway. "What else do you have? Did you talk to any witnesses? Find any relatives, close friends?"

"No, I haven't had a chance for any of that. That's why I don't think even *I* can sell you on page one. It's just too sketchy."

This is a big admission from her. She's page-one-hungry, which makes her a great reporter. She'll dig until she finds out the why of the story, as well as the who, what, where and when.

Clarice ends up writing a brief. We have a discussion cum argument about running the dead guy's name. Her version is that he's an illegal, here for a few months of farm work, and no one outside of the labor camp knows him. I tell her that it doesn't matter, he's been the victim of a crime right here and deserves to be remembered.

I win. She grumbles, and I reschedule the mega-church meeting for tomorrow.

CHAPTER TWO

It's still a month or so before the leaves will start to turn so there's only an occasional nip in the morning air. Mac, my mixed-breed, basic black dog loves his short morning walks this time of year. It's cooler, not raining, lots of his pals are out and now he gets to stay outside while I'm at work. Doggy heaven, but I always worry when my phone rings at night. It may be a neighbor complaining about his barking during the day.

The dense heat of summer is gone but the days continue warm. I choose a lightweight wool skirt and loosely woven top, accessorizing it with a belt slung around my hips. For about a second I consider stilettos, but common sense says, "Don't be stupid," so it's a pair of flats.

At my age—just a bare hair over forty—heels are making a fashion statement, but now I'm judicious about where and when I want to make that statement. A usual workday at the Monroe *Press* isn't a good match.

It's almost 10 a.m. and I've gone through the Bay Area papers, watched a cycle of CNN Headline News and listened to the local TV news as I finished my makeup. There isn't anything that's going to require immediate coverage so I look for the unusual during my ten minute drive to work.

Coming to Monroe was a mistake in so many ways, beginning with Brandon Colby, my ex-husband. After that debacle I stayed long enough to get my daughter, Heather, through high school and launched into college.

The "long enough" was about six years ago and now verging on "too long" but I felt trapped in rising bread dough—a little soft but sticky and clinging. Heather was in her last—oh please let it be her last—year at UC Santa Barbara; I was into the groove at the *Press* and watching my house, my biggest asset, rise in value. If I stick it out here for a few more years, maybe I can retire and work on my book about the late Senator Robert Calvert.

There is something to be said for a ten-minute commute to work. Before I met Brandon I lived and worked in the San Fernando Valley, where just getting to work could be a forty-five minute snarl in traffic.

I stand at the back door of the *Press*, giving myself a few seconds to shift into work mode, then pull the handle. I'm greeted with the muted sounds of phones and keyboards, a signal that all's well. Time to bring up my Funny File, a list of story ideas from overheard conversations, offhand comments, the odd and the bizarre. These make feature stories to round out coverage when there's no pressing news. The staff hates them but readers like them.

Pawing through my calendar, the file, pieces of paper and sticky notes, I run across a jotted note about a wine cellar. That rings a dim bell. I sit with my eyes closed and try to recreate where I was when I heard that.

Right, it was the Labor Day block party. It was a friend of my neighbor talking to a group hovering around the drinks table. Being Labor Day and hot, beer was the drink of choice for most but here, wine is always served. A lot of folks in this area make their living from wine-related activities. Talking about it, drinking it, rating it are good topics to get a party off the ground but this comment was different.

"I heard about a guy who dug into the levee to make a wine cellar." A few gasps, some laughter and one man with a glass of white wine says, "Well, it kept a perfect stable temperature year-round!"

Dredging up that comment, the party came back to me. I'll have to track down the commenter, but a quick call to my neighbor nets me a name and phone number of his friend.

This is right down Gwen's alley. It might be a quirky, light piece about how far wine aficionados would go toward trying to get a *cave* in this area where summer temperatures shoot above 100 degrees. I send her a quick "See me" note.

In less than five minutes she's at my door with question marks in her eyes. "Anything wrong, Amy?"

"Ah, no. Just a feature idea."

I run the party and the comment by her.

"Do you know who the cellar guy is?"

"No. This is going to take some tracking. I have the contact info for the man who made the comment. Not much, but a place to start. When I heard it, I assumed the cellar guy lived in that big development that backs up against the main river levee. I know the Planning Commission is always fielding requests to put in swimming pools and patios so they can enlarge their backyards over there."

Gwen smiles and blows out a soft grunt. She's heard most of these hare-brained ideas over the years. "Those people are always trying to get an extra ten feet of yard. A wine cellar? I haven't heard that one yet. I'll check it out."

At first blush, building a wine cellar in your backyard sounds do-able. Particularly here in California where they don't build houses with basements. The catch in this story is the levee.

Monroe sits in the middle of the Sacramento-San Joaquin Delta, a huge area where the main rivers—the Sacramento from the north, the San Joaquin from the south and the American from the east—come together, turn west and empty into San Francisco Bay. After hundreds of thousands of years, this drainage basin holds some of the most fertile soil on the planet and gold-seekers who didn't make a killing in the streams and mines of the Sierra Nevada made a killing growing food.

One slight flaw. The Delta and the Valley are table-top flat. In the spring snowmelt, so much water tried to flow into the rivers they backed up and overflowed, creating a 200-hundred-mile-long lake for a couple of months each year. About 150 years ago, people began building a series of levees to keep the rivers contained, always a little precarious. A few smaller levees were breached in 1997 and the resulting flood wiped out farming operations on some Delta islands.

So having a homeowner tunnel into the levee at the back of his property for a wine cellar could run from ludicrous to extremely dangerous. I have no idea what Gwen will unearth, but it will be a good story, probably page one worthy.

We're wrapping up our discussion when Clarice almost mows Gwen down at my door. Bless Gwen, she just smiles and sails back to her desk while Clarice continues her conversation. Monologue, because I haven't gotten in a word in yet.

"Great, just great. Here we go again with 'A brief because no one knows him'. What's it gonna take to get these recognized?" She realizes I'm listening, gets slightly pink and pushes on, this time talking *to* me not *at* me. "We have another body in the vineyard."

Now that I'm paying attention, she's taking advantage. "I know, he was just a field hand, an illegal immigrant. The *jefe* IDd this one, too."

"Well, who was he and what do you know?"

"His name was Jesus-something. He was a friend of the first victim, Jorge. They'd come up together every year and follow the crops, but their best one—where they made the most money—was grapes, primarily wine grapes. They'd done it for so many years, they could recognize the different varieties. They had a standing job offer with Carmine

DiFazio."

"DiFazio?"

"Yeah, he owns the vineyard where both were found. Didn't you read my brief?" Her eyes take on a spaniel look. There are two parts to Clarice. Getting a good story and getting praise from everyone who reads it.

"Actually, I didn't read it, I left it for the copy editors. So both of the bodies were found in DiFazio's vineyard?"

The blond nods.

"Which vineyard?"

The DiFazio family has been growing stuff in this area since the 1870s. They were early supporters of building levees and their crops have included cherries, almonds, asparagus, watermelons and walnuts, but their biggest crop has been grapes. Table grapes at times and wine grapes at other times and now they own ten different vineyards throughout the county. They are a well-known early family in Monroe and the current leader, Jules DiFazio, is big in Society here. It's rumored that he has some money riding on the mega-church, although the family members are stalwarts at St. Mary's Catholic Church.

"It's a big one—what two hundred and fifty acres or so?—that's partially along the river. The one they call the Govicche. It's the one where they built the labor camp a few years ago."

[handwritten note: more current migrant worker camps]

CHAPTER THREE

Clarice's news rocks me back a little. The DiFazios have been one of the better farm labor bosses in the area. I know the camp she's talking about. It was a big step up in housing. Each family has a small two-bedroom house and the single men are assigned four to a house. They have running water, indoor bathrooms and electricity. Many of the workers who come back every year move into the same houses so there's a look of permanence, but every year there are a few men who are more migrant, carrying bedrolls and moving on.

Most nights, the workers build a big fire in the outdoor ring and gather to talk, tell stories and pass around bottles. They usually can't afford to go into town and drink in the bars clustered around the rail tracks. *[handwritten: →1 2]*

"Jim...." Clarice catches my look and shuts her mouth so fast she's liable to bite off her tongue.

"You mean Sheriff Dodson?"

Now she's so red she could flag a bull. "Yes, Sheriff Dodson," she says in such a mild voice I feel as though I should look behind her for the ventriloquist.

"What you and the sheriff do on your personal and private time is none of my business and I don't want to know. But here, or at the cops, you'd better watch yourself. If any hint of a personal life between you leaks out, you'll get taken off the cops beat so fast you won't have time to type your byline. And if the town gets wind of the sheriff fooling around with a reporter, he'll have challengers coming out of the woodwork."

"I know Amy, that just slipped out. You're right. I was talking to him right before I came in and didn't take the time to shift gears."

"Maybe you'd better get an automatic, then. What did Sheriff Dodson say?"

She regains a bit of composure. "He thinks that the two guys were both murdered by someone they'd fought with earlier. Maybe they got wasted and all got into a fight. Now the third guy is picking them off."

"If that's so, not worth much of a story until they catch the third guy."

"Well, yeah." She's pensive. "That'll probably never happen. If it's someone from the camp, he's probably already in Fresno, hired out to one of the big growers. The murders will go stone cold."

"Let's do another brief. You can throw in a quote from one of the sheriff's guys and maybe try to get DiFazio's foreman to say something. Other than that, I think it's over."

She nods in agreement and starts to leave when a thought hits me. "Clarice, what do you know about the DiFazios, specifically Jules?"

"Not much. Probably what everybody else knows. They're rich, they've been here forever, they grow a lot of grapes."

"When you have some time, see what else you can dig up. Where'd they get their start, are they really a silent partner in the mega-church, have they applied for Williamson Act withdrawal? But be careful and use tact. Don't stomp on Gwen's toes and be wary of Roberts. I just want some background and you're a great researcher."

Mollified, her red recedes and a smile lurks at the corners of her mouth. Clarice loves compliments, and she probably deserves more than I give her.

I jot myself a note on a sticky. Govicche? DiFazo? The story that everybody in town knows is that the DiFazios bought out the Govicches at the beginning of Prohibition. The Govicches were growing an old grape, good for wine but not suited for fresh table grapes. They were selling some for sacramental wine, and folks were buying them fresh to make their own wine at home, but it wasn't enough to make the vineyard pay.

With the DiFazios' other agricultural holdings, they could keep the vineyard producing at a minimum and hope for better times.

The note gets stuck on the side of my monitor. When I have a chunk of time, I'll visit Nancy, my friend the reference librarian.

This mega-church is making me crazy. Today's meeting is on the same track and I can't keep my mind on it.

I tune back in as Don Roberts says, "If the mayor is really a member of the congregation it should be the city hall reporter's responsibility to cover this."

It's an old refrain from him. He takes every chance he can to foist his work off on somebody else and this looks like a slam-dunk to him.

Here, in the heart of California's Central Valley, the non-denominational evangelical movement is growing along with the area.

This whole story is a DBI, Dull But Important. Monroe is either a big town or a small city and the population has grown over the past decade, fueled by people fleeing the expense and congestion of the Bay Area, less than a hundred miles to the west. And a lot of people are leaving the liberal Bay Area behind to find like minds in the more conservative valley.

With the new population, the heart is changing from a conservative, settled agricultural base to a mixture of commuters and developers. Land that used to house crops now houses houses—big houses. Because ag land was relatively cheap, and the economy was booming, developers laid out small lots and built HUGE homes. Transplants could afford a 3,000 square-foot house, unthinkable in San Francisco or the Peninsula or the East Bay. This issue affects both the older residents and the newer people living in McMansions. What's at stake is the plowing under of five acres of old vineyard, some of the last ag land in the city limits.

I'd been digging my nails into my hands to stay awake, again. In my now-conscious state, Roberts' whine drills into me like a slow-speed dentist, making my molars hurt.

"Again, Don, you're the religion reporter. This church expansion is *your* story. Gwen will handle the political angle, but you are the point person. You have to have an overview of the whole project. If something skews a different way, you have to understand how it will affect the entire project."

"Skew? What skew?" Roberts is getting truculent.

"I don't know. That's why we're here." I look at Gwen who placidly nods. She and Sally, the education reporter, are both pros who've chosen Monroe for the duration and believe that their work makes this a better place to live.

Gwen takes the lead. "We've heard all the rumors from it's going to be able to accommodate 4,000 in the auditorium, to it's going to house a K-12 Christian school, busing kids in from all over the county. If the auditorium is that big, it'll be the biggest place in Monroe to have any event. If it's a school, there'll be a lot of noise from a big patch of land that's only vines now."

Not for the first time, Gwen's quiet voice of reason calms the building tension. She's here because there are tax implications with this project. Ag land is taxed at a low rate, but a church pays no property tax. Current property owners and local sales taxes will pay for police protection and other services.

Sally's education beat might take a hit, too. If a few hundred kids get pulled out of the local school system to go to a new private school, the district will lose the money it gets from the state for each child.

Roberts is off again. "City Hall and the schools are the ones affected by this church. I still don't see why I have to cover this."

"Enough! This is the last time I'm saying it. You're the religion reporter and this is a church. It's your story. Why is the evangelical movement growing here? Will this be only for locals or are they planning to attract other people? Look at the impact the Crystal Cathedral has had in Orange County. There are a lot of issues here and we have to tell people about all of them—the good and the bad."

Luis the photographer is twitching. Excitement? Frustration? He looks like a kindergartener trying to get the teacher's attention. "What do you want pictures of? I can go shoot the vineyard now."

"No, no pictures of empty land. Shoot speakers at the Planning Commission. With luck, there'll be protestors with signs. If the zoning goes through, shoot the bulldozers ripping out the vines. Either way, someone's going to feel shorted."

The group gathers up their stuff and heads out again to work their contacts. Whichever way the decision goes, we'll have comment and reaction from the community.

Clarice's body-in-the-vineyard is another reminder that harvest is beginning. The food produced here is known around the country. Cherries, pears, nuts, asparagus, peaches, apricots, milk and dairy. Hands down, though, this part of the Valley is known for its grapes and vineyards.

North is the Napa Valley, with the Napa and Sonoma wineries that challenge the European varietals beloved by wine aficionados. South are the vineyards and wineries that make basic California table wines. Monroe is the bulls-eye, the middle that produces grapes that get shipped off to the north and also feeding a couple of local well-known wineries.

The local roads are busy now with grape gondolas, funny-shaped trucks whose trailers can be up-tilted sideways to dump grapes into the crushers.

With the harvest just beginning, Luis needs to take the annual picture of a local priest blessing the first crush. And now the smell of money comes drifting through the windows at night—the smell of the crush and fermentation.

I sit back and let my mind wander to Clarice's body in the vineyard. The growers won't let the investigation slow down the harvest. Whoever that guy was, he isn't getting weeks of mourning.

Stories get written, phone calls made, reporters stick their heads in to ask "How long do you want this," "I couldn't find anybody to give me a quote," "Is it better to lead with the vote?" The last one is from Steve, a new general assignment reporter who's covered a nearby school district board meeting.

I'm giving him different assignments—hard news as well as features—to see if he's better at one than the other. So far, he's better at writing briefs, those small page two one and two paragraph stories announcing meetings or following up on unremarkable crimes or verdicts. If a guy arrested two years ago for aggravated assault (he stabbed another guy after a night of drinking; the victim survived) finally gets sentenced to a few years with the sentence knocked down to time served in the county jail, it's not worth the time and trouble to do more than record his sentence.

These are the small stories that we run as briefs because we cover everything. Anyone can do them; it takes one call to the judge's clerk to get the sentencing facts, a half hour or so researching the original crime stories and a few more minutes to write. It's a way of getting as much news as possible into an ever-shrinking news-hole, the space that's available for news, left over after the ads are placed.

Even the New York Times runs briefs. Theirs tend to be about people charged in a sex-ring across four states, where ours are about the theft of five cows. It's only a matter of scale and community interest.

I've tried him on the school board meeting. There's potential for interest on this one. Tucked away in the agenda is a vote to shorten the school day by ten minutes. This is actually a big deal because the state mandates how many hours a year a child has to be in school. The board is looking at it as a way to shave the personnel budget.

"Why would you start the story with the vote?" I want Steve to think about it. He wrinkles his sandy eyebrows which makes his twenty-something face look like a toddler who's just had a toy taken away.

"Well, the football team is a big deal and there were about fifteen parents there wanting to talk about it..." His instincts are right, any time fifteen people turn out for a school board meeting, it merits a story.

"What about the agenda item to shorten the school day?"

"The board just assigned that to a study group and nobody protested." he says, looking as though he may have missed the bus entirely.

"There were fifteen people at the meeting? Find one of them, and interview him or her about why they all turned out. That's your lede. And talk to Sally about the shorter day."

Suddenly the cops monitor breaks out in excited babble and Clarice stands up so fast I'm afraid she'll pass out from the blood draining from her head. Her eyes are squinched and she's making frantic squiggles in her notebook, so far gone she doesn't hear me.

"Clarice, CLAR...what's going on?"

"They've got an overturned grape gondola and it's closed part of the freeway. I'm outta here..." trails behind her like autumn fog as she slams out the door.

CHAPTER FOUR

I wonder when the other shoe will drop. The monitor is squawking and I hear a lot of sirens. City police, county sheriff and local fire are responding. Then I hear "Ambulance on the way."

I call Clarice's cell, needing to talk to her as soon as possible. It's not just a nosy question, I have to figure out how much space and play this story requires. It's on a freeway off ramp which means part of the freeway may be blocked. They're calling for an ambulance, which means someone's hurt or dead. This is an incident that affects a fair number of people. We can't just ignore it.

It seems like hours before she calls back. In the meantime, I tell Luis, my photographer, to be ready to roll and send a note to Sandy on the copy desk to hold some local pages. We're as ready as we can be.

When she calls, it's bad. The trailer tipped off an elevated freeway connector ramp. The truck itself fell onto the freeway lanes below, smashing two cars while most of its load of grapes spilled out on the ramp. Both roads are closed and the CHP is already on the scene, trying to direct traffic into a makeshift lane they've opened on the shoulder.

"I know they've called for a Medi-Vac helicopter. They'll have to shut down all northbound lanes to land it." Clarice's voice is excited. She knows this will be a page one story.

"How many injured?"

"It looks like two injured and maybe one dead." Her voice drops a little. "The cars smushed by the truck are pretty bad."

"OK, Luis's on his way. Are you somewhere you can get out?"

I hear her sigh. "Yep, I parked on the shoulder of the freeway. Once it's opened, I can drive down to the next ramp and loop back. I'll look for Luis. It's going to be a while."

Now it's my turn to sigh. "I'll tell Sandy to hold page one. Get back as soon as you can, but take care."

Truck accidents are inevitable here. With the Central Valley producing the lion's share of agricultural products in the U.S., trucks haul most of the year—livestock, chickens, fruits and vegetables, cotton. Late summer and fall is when the traffic peaks with tomatoes, peaches and grapes in our part of the valley. There's always some squished fruit on the freeways, baking into the asphalt until the rains start and turn it into a slick mush again.

I'm particularly concerned about this one and Clarice. She's always ready to go but a couple of years ago she went out to cover a truck that slammed into an abutment of an overcrossing. It was a single vehicle accident. The truck caught fire. Gas that spilled across the freeway caught fire. The responders couldn't get to the trucker.

Clarice listened to his screams until they stopped.

She's told me she still hears the screams when she gets to a truck accident.

And sometimes at night.

After Sandy's alerted and Luis's gone, I read the school board story. It's hard to keep my mind on it. Steve rewrote it, leading off with an interview with the father of the school's football quarterback. He pleaded with the board not to cut sports, probably because he saw football as his kid's best chance to go on to college.

"Much better," I told Steve. "It personalizes the meeting, brings the reader into someone's life."

He ducks his head, trying to conceal a grin, but he glances at me and realized I'm smiling too. We share a smile and a nod until my phone rings.

"Well, one dead, one Medi-vac'd, one transported by ambulance. The truck driver is OK, he's the one in the ambulance. Maybe a broken arm and being checked for any other injuries." She can be terse when needed.

"Who's dead?" A grisly question that needs an answer.

"The dead guy and the seriously injured one were in the first car that the truck landed on. The second car sort of ran into the combo car-truck. Air bags went off, no serious injuries, the driver was treated at the scene and released."

"Who is everybody? Where are they from?"

"I'm getting there, Amy. They won't release names of the dead guy, or the serious injuries, until they notify next-of-kin. Should be tonight."

"What names do you have? Any cause?"

"The treated-at-the-scene is a woman from Stockton. She was driving home from a shopping trip. The truck driver is Manual Oropezo. He's a resident alien."

Hmmm. So far we're best going with the traffic jam resulting from the accident. Before I can get the question out, Clarice says "The woman who was just behind the second car barely missed the whole thing. She swerved into the median and kicked up a big dust cloud. That's probably why there weren't more cars involved, they saw the dust and figured something's wrong."

"Did you talk to her?"

There's dead silence on the phone. "Are you still there?"

"Of course I'm still here. And yes, of course I talked to her."

Oops.

"She's a nurse at the VA hospital in Sacramento. Coming

home from her shift. She lives in Monroe."

"Great! And she wasn't hurt?"

"Nope. In fact she helped out. She's the first 911 caller. Got the woman ahead of her out of her car so she didn't get slammed into. Ran to the really smashed car and talked to the guys until fire rescue arrived. Then stayed until everybody got carted off to the hospital. They're calling her a hero."

"Better and better! Did Luis get a shot of her?"

"Yep, while she was talking to the ambulance crew."

We have a great, positive page one package. A fatal truck accident is sad. Hopefully it hammers safe driving home. This one though has survivors and a hometown hero.

"OK, the mainbar is the accident. Do they have a cause yet? A nice sidebar on the nurse. Can Luis get a shot of her at home?"

"She doesn't want a big to-do. She's mandated to offer aid if she stops. Until the flight nurse got there, our nurse was the highest medical authority at the scene. She thought she might have to go with the ambulance."

"Well, what about the cause? Any early ideas?"

"They're not finished yet. They've just found a wrecker large enough to haul the mess off the freeway and they're still scraping and hosing the grape goo. They did find a couple of blown tires, but don't know if that's a cause or effect. We'll have to follow-up later when they announce the dead guy's name and pin down a cause."

I'm sending a note to Sandy as Clarice gives me more details. We can have a story and two photos on page one, with a jump to the back and the sidebar.

We're not a "if it bleeds, it leads" operation but when this kind of incident happens, we need to let readers know. I'm jotting down notes for follow-up when Clarice stops me short.

"What was that?" I'm not sure I heard her.

"I said the truck belongs to DiFazio Vineyards. I wonder if this is gonna affect their harvest?"

CHAPTER FIVE

Clarice asks a good question. Losing two harvest crew members shouldn't affect their field teams, but that plus a loss of grape gondolas and a truck may make the DiFazios shuffle hard.

Grape gondolas are specialty trailers, designed with hooks at the ends to be picked up and dumped sideways into the crush machines at the wineries and you don't just order them online. Plus, anybody else with gondolas is using them 24/7 to haul their grapes NOW.

Commodity crops, especially high-end commodity crops like wine grapes, won't hang around waiting. They're scientifically monitored for sugar and when it's optimum, they're off the vines in a heartbeat and on the way to get crushed, smushed and otherwise stomped on for their juice.

She's back in the office and I eye her speculatively. The DiFazios' troubles can make a good story, one the major metros in both Northern and Southern California might pick up. And maybe even the New York Times if it can get framed right. Wine in general and California wine in particular has become a Big Deal and our little area is being watched closely.

She's reading over her notes in my office doorway and

feels me looking at her.

"What? What do you have in mind? I hate that look."

"Nothing, maybe. I don't know. I'm thinking there's a story here about the highs and lows of farming. Grape growers can make a lot of money. What's their gamble? Weather, labor, pests, it's a long list. I wonder what makes them keep at it."

"Humph." She rolls her eyes at me. "Money and prestige. Look at all the money from celebs that got dumped into Napa and Sonoma Counties. Look at that soap, what was its name, Falcon-something? Made grape growing look like a tidy garden with jealousy."

"Falcon Crest. That was a long time ago, what twenty, twenty-five years?"

"Yeah, but those images stay with people." She gives a snarky little laugh. "At least those fashions went away." Her eyes narrow. "Wait a minute, you aren't going to have me go talk to growers and wineries, are you?"

Clarice is not at her best when dealing with what passes for the upper crust. She's brash, blunt and slightly disheveled—perfect for a police chase but a little off-putting for a tea party. That's why she excels with the cops. She speaks their language and relates to their customers.

"I don't know if you'd be the best one to do it. I'm still thinking."

Hoo-boy, that got a rise. She swivels back into my office with her earnest face on. "What do you mean? I could do a perfect job. Do you think I can't research and write an in-depth feature?"

"Of course you can, but what I'm thinking might require a lot of time. I don't want you to give up your beat for weeks."

She blanches. "Weeks? No I don't want to do that."

"Maybe we can get a team together for this."

"What kind of a team? Who would I work with? There are some people out there," she vaguely waves at the newsroom, "I don't want to work with."

"I know Clar. I can probably name them. This is an idea. Maybe I'll do some of the research." Clarice and I have worked on big stories together and we both still have all our skin.

"Well, that might work. I've gotta get this accident story written. I wonder if they'll release the names yet." Her jet-stream-of-consciousness sucks the air out of my office as she heads to her desk.

What have I put myself into? A somewhat idle comment, but the more I think about it, the more it makes sense. There's a lot of information about wine, vineyards, wineries but not everyone writes about wine from the grunt-work perspective.

The air has a slight hint of fall tang as I head to the library. I need to talk to Nancy, do some research, see if this idea is worth any time investment.

I ease my way into her office, shaking off the clerk who tags along like a terrier, nipping at my heels and saying, "Do you have an appointment?" It's a little rude, but I don't have a lot of time.

Nancy looks up from a big and old book she's spread across her desk. "Well, hi there. Come on in. Oh, you're already in!" She smiles and pushes her glasses up on her head. "You must be after something; it's late afternoon and you're usually up to your hips in it by now."

Having a friend like Nancy, one who knows you almost as well as you know yourself, is golden. We bonded instantly when I arrived in Monroe with a daughter in tow who made fast friends with Nancy's daughter. The girls are both in college now at different ends of the state. They've drifted apart but Nancy and I are firm.

I shake my head. "I am, but I also want to bounce something off of you. You heard about the truck crash?"

Now it's her turn to shake, so I recap Clarice's afternoon, ending with the kicker about the DiFazios. She blows out a breath. "They *have* had a streak of bad luck this harvest. Why are you dragging me into it?"

"Dragging? No. But right to the point. I want to find out more about the DiFazios, the Govicches, the history of wine grapes here."

"Oh sure, and you'd like this PhD history thesis what, in about an hour?"

"No, tomorrow is fine," I slide a look at her and we both start to giggle.

"I know I'm pushing you. What I really need is for you to give me some recommendations, some paths to follow. If this project works, it'll take a while to flesh it out."

"Let me think about it. Come back tomorrow. Hmmm..." I can tell something is frothing at the front of her mind. "One of the first things I'd recommend is a visit to the Shields Library at UC Davis and head to the Viticulture and Enology collection. You might get yourself to the Wine Institute in San Francisco, as well. Maybe you can combine it with a visit with that friend of yours." She's raising her eyebrows and now she actually winks at me!

"Wait a minute, you're Marian the Librarian! What are you suggesting?"

Nancy is recently divorced and hasn't started dating again. I'm thinking she may never. She felt seriously burned when her husband of almost twenty-five years announced one day that he was gay and had fallen in love with another man. It took a lot of wine, late nights, boxes of tissues and some professional counseling before she understood that it wasn't her fault. She could have become the Perfect Wife and it wouldn't matter.

Her sanity is hard-won and she's likely to stay calm reading, gardening and rescuing abandoned small dogs.

"Nothing, nothing. It just seemed you had a great time with him and could maybe use some more."

"You're right." I can feel pink creeping up my neck. "I did, and I think he's up for it again. At least, this will give me a business agenda we can discuss...maybe over dinner and drinks!"

"I'll start rounding up background on the families and call you in a couple of days when I have something." She pulls her glasses down and I head back to work, remembering the last weekend I spent with Phil.

Definite possibility.

CHAPTER SIX

I'm not moving warp-speed ahead on DiFazio-Govicche research.

Things kind of fizzled out after the gondola accident. Clarice found a new shiny object—two bodies in the grease pit of a speedy oil change place—and was bugging the cops about it.

"The Sheriff, Jim, has pulled his undercover guys to work on this," she says during a swing into my office, her "drive-thru" way of keeping me apprised. "I think he thinks there's a drug connection here."

"And is that a problem? A conspiracy?"

She's slowly shaking her head, coming back to now. "No, I'm just wondering if this is going to turn into a bigger picture, a raid on the dealers story. They haven't given me a lot beyond IDs and cause of death."

"And these are?"

She flips her notebook open. "The dead guys are Jackson Smythe and Ricky Bob Thomas. Both from the L.A. area, no local address or employers that they've found. Both shot twice in the head. No shells recovered. Sounds sorta pro to me."

I'm thinking the same thing. We really don't have tons of

murders here, but a few times a year there's a beef over drugs—buying, selling, turf—and someone ends up dead. Not drive-by shootings, not a lot of gang activity, but some residents of the nearby rural areas supplement their income cooking meth. This causes explosions, fires and kids ending up in foster care because mom and dad are in jail on child endangerment charges.

"Well, keep on it and let me know," I say as her cell rings.

"Yeah?" She's nodding at the phone. "Who told you that?" Now she shifts her phone to her left ear, drops her notebook on my desk and leans over, taking notes. "How long ago was that? Jeez! OK, thanks." The phone clicks shut and she swipes it and her notebook in her purse, heading out the door.

"Hey, wait a minute! What's going on?" Her conversation is cryptic enough that it could be personal, but I doubt it.

"That was one of the women at the labor camp. The found Angel's body. Gotta go, the cops are on their way."

"Angel, the hooker Angel? Our Angel?"

Clarice turns to me long enough to say, "Our Angel. There's something funny going on. I'll call as soon as I get some info." This time she almost mows down Steve as she makes it out of my office at a speed-walk.

Steve is stunned. He stands motionless, his chin on his chest and hurt welling up in his eyes like a dog that's been kicked

"Don't take it personally. When she gets a tip, she acts first. She's never actually run anybody down. Were you coming in to see me?" I play my calm, mom-ish voice, not wanting him to get peeved at Clarice.

"Uh, yes." He closes his mouth. "But now...oh right. I was coming in to see if you had anything you wanted me to do." The almost-collision with Clarice short-circuited him momentarily.

"Perfect timing. I don't know the details, but Angel's body was just found at the labor camp. You can start pulling some background."

Now his open mouth is an accompaniment to his stunned expression.

"Who's Angel? What background?"

Damn. I'm getting Clarice-ish. Assuming everyone understands my mental shorthand.

"Sorry, I forget you haven't been here forever." I wave him in and to a chair. "You've probably heard that we have a group of hookers, prostitutes, down by the packing sheds and the bars. They move into town with the crops and the grape harvest is their big season. Angel is our very own. She's from the valley, showed up a few years ago and just stayed. Clarice did a feature on her, plus she's had a few run-ins."

He's still stunned. His J-school degree didn't prep him for this. "Clarice did a feature on a hooker?"

"A couple of years ago, yes. She's always looking for a quirky clip. Go pull up any info and read the feature. If it's 'funny' as Clarice said, we'll need a background piece. You can write it."

He stands up and does a modified zombie-walk out of my office. If he doesn't find enough information or treat Angel with the reverence Clarice will demand, this may be a misstep. On the other hand, working on an off-beat story with a connection to the cops beat might be enough to light a fire.

I put in a call to Sheriff Dodson, not to circumvent Clarice's relationship but to find out what they're doing. His secretary says he's out of the office, but she can put me through to his voicemail. Ha, wonder where he is? The secretary sure won't tell.

Clarice finally calls. It is Angel and she is dead. "Murdered?"

"I'd sure say so." The blond is subdued. "Looks like her throat was cut with a grape knife, you know the ones with the hook at the end.. A lot of blood on the ground."

"You saw her?"

"They were still taking crime scene pictures when I got here. I didn't get real close, but the blood was obvious. Jim, uh, the Sheriff, is here. I'm going to go ask him why he didn't call me."

Oh God. "Wait, Clarice, don't piss him off! His phone isn't on speed-dial to you every time he gets called out."

There's a thin and symbiotic line between the press and the police. We need each other and we need to trust each other and starting an argument accusing them of covering up isn't the tack to take. Whatever is going on personally between Clarice and Jim Dodson can't slop over to their professional relationship.

"Well, thanks Amy. I know that. It's just that they know I've covered the two field guys and I'd kinda thought they'd know I was interested in Angel. I guess my feelings are hurt."

What an admission from Clarice! I'm proud of her for working that out. "I know, Clar, you're always on top of things and it does feel personal when you think they've left you out. What's the next step?"

"They're putting her in a body bag now. I'm going to talk to Maria, she's the woman who called me. Then I'm going to find some of the guys who were with her. I should be back by six or so."

"Good. I've got Steve researching background. I've assigned him a sidebar on Angel, primarily from your feature."

"Steve? Well, it could be worse. I'll talk to him when I get in."

This is way past coincidence. The most visible hooker in town, the one who even the cops had a soft spot for, found dead, murdered, at the labor camp for DiFazio workers.

What was she doing out there? She had her own place in town, a studio tucked away in an alley where she did business. And she usually left the farm workers to the transient hookers who followed the crops.

Well, Clarice knows this is going on page one.

And the research on the wine families needs to get brought to the front burner.

Maybe an email to Phil is in order.

CHAPTER SEVEN

We seem to have a body epidemic. Clarice revels in her "Angel of Death" nickname. I call Jim Dodson. The phone shunts me to voicemail and I leave a message, wondering if I'll get a call back.

I'm not going to pick up and leave for a drive to Davis, I need to stay here and keep tabs on Angel's murder, but I do begin a web search. Like all good searches, it begins to run in tangential paths. My first ask is for DiFazio and I get quite a few hits, mostly their site and PR for their wines. They seem to be accumulating commendations and awards since Jules took over management.

A reference to appellation piques my interest. I know that this is a geographic area that grows grapes and those grapes command premium prices. I know there are lots of appellations in California.

I know Monroe had earned an appellation and now I find out that it was Jules DiFazio who pushed for it. A trip to Google and I discover that appellations and wines fall under the purview of Bureau of Alcohol, Tobacco and Firearms. Odd, this is the Department of Justice, not Agriculture, where other crops are. Then I flash back to the moonshine days and running battles with Revenuers. Alcohol is heavily taxed. And wine is an alcohol.

It just seems a little bizarre that highly-rated and expensive wines favored by the connoisseurs are regulated by the same folks who were at Waco and Ruby Ridge.

For a wine to have an appellation on its label, eighty-five percent of the grapes in the wine have to be grown in that region. An appellation certainly makes DiFazio's grapes worth more, but they don't make wine, just grow grapes. Their grapes get shipped to wineries around Northern California, many of them to the premiere wineries in Napa and Sonoma counties. I'll ask Jules about why he pushed for an appellation.

I'm making notes when Jim Dodson calls back.

"What can I do for you, Amy?" His voice is regaining some of its urban tenor as he takes on the role of sheriff in a much larger county. When we first met, he was the sheriff of San Juan County, a small, rural area in the Sierra foothills east of Monroe. As we got to know each other, we discovered people in common, including my first husband, Vinnie Hobbes.

Jim knows the story of Vinnie's death during a high-speed chase. He doesn't treat me with kid gloves, but the knowledge has built a bond of trust between us and he'll give me background, knowing I won't burn him. And there's always whatever's going on with Clarice.

"It just struck me that we suddenly seem to have lots of bodies. Do you think there's something going on?"

He laughs. "Going on? Like an outbreak of death? I'm not sure what you mean."

"Well, we had the two field workers, then the guy who died in the accident and now Clarice is off chasing the two guys who were found in the grease pit. And I'm not even talking about Angel. We don't usually have this many suspicious deaths in Monroe."

"Oh, Amy, I depend on you being the voice of reason. Are you seeing some kind of conspiracy? Maybe a rash of dead bodies that my department can solve right before I run for office?"

"That's gruesome! No, I wasn't thinking that." The hair on my arms stands at attention. "More, I guess, that these aren't our home-grown baddies."

Now his voice tenses. "What have you been hearing? Who have you and Clarice been talking to?"

"No one, nothing. Nothing out of the ordinary. I'm just getting an itch at the back of my brain. Is there some tie in that I'm missing?"

"Well I'll tell *you*, I don't know of any tie-in. The two field workers...we really think that's just a beef between them. Angel may or may not tie in, it's too early yet to see a pattern. The accident? It's just an accident and the CHP has jurisdiction. They haven't found anything that they're telling me. It's the luck of the draw that DiFazio's truck was involved.

"The guys in the grease pit? Off the record and as background, the feds are involved here. DEA has been watching those guys and some others. Primarily cooking and distributing meth, but some cross-border traffic may be involved."

I'm ticking the bodies off as he's talking. "Well, that still leaves three dead people you're responsible for. And all three have the DiFazio link as well."

"That's true," Dodson says quietly. "We're working things now. There isn't a lot at the scenes. All three were killed—I wouldn't call it stabbed—by grape pruning and harvesting knives. Grape pruning knives all have a hook at the end, they slash more than they stab. I think some of the workers use small machetes, but those will take off a finger or your hand, not stab you, same with the clippers. We're testing as many tools as we can find for blood residue. And no, nothing yet."

"Has Clarice..."

Before I can even get the question out, Dodson says "I haven't told Clarice any of this yet. As soon as we get the testing done, I'm going to sit down with her. I'd prefer it staying as background for now."

Are things coming to a halt on the Jim-Clarice road? I don't know if he knows that I know that he and Clarice are a sometime item, but I'm sure not going to mention it. I want to keep it in the "Don't ask, don't tell" file. Too much knowledge can be uncomfortable.

"I didn't call to ask how the vineyard bodies are doing, just to get a suspicion—no that's too strong—a trace of concern on the table. As background for you, I'm toying with the idea of assigning a story on the number of bodies lately."

"I'm not going to tell you how to do your job, Amy, but my preference would be that you don't do a story like that."

My back goes up immediately. He certainly isn't going to tell me how to do my job. "And why is that?" I hope I'm keeping the anger out of my voice.

"Primarily so we don't get inundated by the copy-cats and the confessors. When the media plays a murder big, we always have that contingent calling with a confession. These are the ones with a few loose hinges, but we have to check every one out. Takes up a lot of manpower for nothing."

I concede he has a point. It isn't in our best interests to swamp his department with a lot of dead-end leads. At the same time, I won't let any of the bodies get swept under the rug.

"We won't do a story...yet. Clarice can count, so I'm pretty sure she's going to come at you with this same question." I'm quiet for a moment, then barge ahead. "There's something else I wanted to ask you about."

Now the quiet is on his end. He clears his throat. "What's that?"

I hear tension in his voice. I may have come at this the wrong way but now I've begun.

"I've never talked to anyone about this, but Vinnie insisted I have a gun and he taught me how to shoot. After he was killed, I didn't want a gun in the house—for his memory and because of Heather—so I gave it to his department. Now I'm thinking about it again."

"Does this have anything to do with our body count?"

"No...yes...well, maybe. Monroe is a quiet small town, city, but living alone and watching Clarice pick up on every crime, I guess I'm concerned."

"What do you want me to do? Why are you telling me this?"

"I'm not sure. I don't know if I want to own a gun, but I would like to go to a shooting range to see how I feel about it."

Silence. Then, "That I can do. It's probably best if we go to the indoor range next to Jack's Guns. Do you know where that is? I can carve out sometime tomorrow at noon."

"I do. I can meet you there. Please don't tell anyone about this, I really don't like guns and most people know that. I don't want it broadcast that I've changed my mind."

This is a scary step I've taken. Not only will it bring back vivid memories of Vinnie but the idea of shooting a gun for the first time in more than fifteen years makes me nervous. I'm still not sure why I even thought of it.

CHAPTER EIGHT

Going to a shooting range in the middle of the day strikes me as an offbeat lunch date. The Sheriff is already there looking at the gun displays when I come in and he waves me over.

"I've told Jack we just want to practice with a few handguns."

Although I've known Jim Dodson for a few months, I've always seen him in his administrative and managerial role. I sort of forget he's a sworn officer and usually carries a gun. He takes on a different persona around all these firearms and I'm a bit intimidated.

"Do you know if you want to buy one?"

"Not today." I'm shivery and try not to let it show. "I'm not even sure if I ever want one."

The gun store stuns me. There are handguns, rifles, shotguns and even an Uzi on display, hanging from the walls and laid out in long cases. There's even a big case of ammunition. Plus displays of holsters, gun cases, gun safes, cleaning supplies and some things I think are gun locks. I feel as though I've stepped into a different universe.

Dodson senses my hesitancy. "Jack, let's try a few so she

can get the feel of them. Let's start with a Glock."

A Glock? Isn't that what spies use? Dodson and Jack are engrossed in a conversation that I'm not following, tossing around words like Ruger and Heckler & Koch, and Kahr Arms. I figure out that these are different gun makers. They have preferences, I don't. They finally decide that the 9mm Glock will be the best to start me with. They lead me through a door to the range itself and load up the magazine. There's one other person already here and the noise is deafening until Jack hands me a pair of sound deadening ear muffs. They smash down my hair, but the silence is blissful.

The range Vinnie took me to was outdoors, but the setup is the same—a long counter separated by partitions and a set of targets. These are strung on clothes-line like wires so you can reel them in and see where your shot went. Unlike Vinnie's range where the target was a body outline, these are traditional bulls-eyes, much better.

I pick up the gun and it's heavier than I expect. Dodson stands behind me and puts his arms around me, holding my hands.

"Use two hands. Don't pull the trigger, squeeze it. There'll be a kick, so prepare yourself."

He steps away and I'm alone, trying to aim down the short barrel of the gun. I have the bulls-eye sighted and I slowly squeeze the trigger. The sound startles me, the kick is strong and the barrel goes zooming up to point at the roof. I don't think this is right.

I glance over and both of them are holding in a grin.

"Try again," Dodson says. "The magazine holds ten rounds."

By the time I'm at the last of the rounds, I'm able to steady the gun enough so that I actually hit the target—the paper part, not the bulls-eye. They put a fresh magazine in and after it's empty I'm able to hold it steady and hit inside the bulls-eye. My last shot is just outside the center and I'm ready to call it quits. My arms are a little shaky from holding them at shoulder height and there's some numbness in my hands but I'm pleased that I'm not jerking and am hitting *almost* where I aim.

"Are you going to buy one?" Dodson is picking up various models Jack has set out.

"Not today. They still bring back memories of Vinnie. But thanks so much for bringing me, Sheriff Dodson. And Jack, thank you for letting me try the Glock. If I decide to buy a gun, this seems to be a good choice."

Outside, Dodson and I stand and chat for a couple of minutes. We're a little chary with one another. I don't tell him that I'm still thinking about a story on the mounting body count, nor do I tell him I've begun some research on the DeFazios. He doesn't tell me if his department's dug up any more information on Angel's death, so we're even.

I reach out to shake his hand and he takes it in both of his. "I understand why you have concerns, after Vinnie. If you do decide, give me a call and I'll come with you."

"Thanks Jim, that's a very generous offer," I say, dropping his hand and digging for keys in my purse.

It's been an educational lunch hour, not a nourishing one. I pick up a salad to eat at my desk and make a nail appointment. This nail salon in Monroe functions like a men's club used to—you can pick up all sorts of gossip cum information. What I pick up this afternoon is a lot of chat about who's going to the DiFazios' annual end-of harvest party. And I manage to wangle an invitation from a DiFazio sister-in-law, a woman who knew Brandon Colby, my ex-husband, well.

Social life in Monroe is iffy. Brandon was well-known and well-liked in Monroe and our wedding was a big, splashy affair. When he left me to move to Chicago with his new, pregnant girlfriend, the whole town knew that as well. He's still one of the town's fair-haired boys, but they can't ignore me, primarily because of my job, so I get a few invitations every year. My current private social life is in San Francisco with Phil, and I want to keep these separate.

Just before deadline, Clarice rolls in looking like a storm. She slams her purse, cell, keys down on her desk and rumbles into my office.

"The feds! Those two guys in the grease pit were connected to the DEA. Do you know how hard it is to get information from the feds? I can't get any help from the Sheriff's office. I have a call into the FBI, the DEA and every alphabet soup agency I can think of. What do you think my chances of hearing back are? Nil! Zilch!"

I haven't seen her this upset since...well, since a Sacramento TV reporter broke a story on the so-called Speed Freak Killers in neighboring San Joaquin County. Clarice had been researching the murders to do an update on the search for bodies when the story hit the screen. That time she was so upset she ended up in tears of frustration, which made her even angrier.

"Calm down, Clarice. I'm sure you'll get a call back. Have you talked to the Sherriff's office about this yet?" I'm not going to tell her that I've already been told this by Dodson.

"The Public Information Officer told me he couldn't talk about it and the Sherriff was out all afternoon and hasn't returned my calls."

She spins around and stomps back to her desk, determined to salvage some kind of story about this murder. I've only known Clarice for the past few years and have seen her upset several times, but this seems blown out of all proportion.

I'm shutting everything down when she taps at my door.

"Have a minute?"

This is not a usual Clarice approach. I say "Sure," thinking she might be offering me an apology for her earlier outburst.

She comes in and closed the door. Uh-oh.

"I want to talk to you about Jim Dodson, the Sheriff." Her voice is low and a little shaky.

"What about him?"

"Well...umm..."

She finally looks me in the eye and says, "I saw you and Jim Dodson holding hands outside of Jack's gun store this afternoon. This is awkward, but I just want to know if you're interested in him. I know you guys have a common background and I don't want..."

This has to be uncomfortable for her because she stops mid-sentence and looks at me. I'm sure she can see the amazement.

"Oh Clarice, this is how rumors start! You've jumped to the wrong conclusion and I'm so sorry!"

I tell her the story of why it looked like the Sheriff and I were holdings hands at lunch time. "I don't want anyone to know about this. I always get on my soapbox about gun control and if anybody thinks I might buy a gun, well I just don't want to go down that road. Particularly since I'm not even sure. And no, I'm not interested in Sheriff Dodson beyond professionally."

Now the blush begins in her chest and zooms its way to the roots of her hair.

"Thanks, Amy. I don't mean to be so stupid about this. I don't have any idea what's going to happen and I know I'm letting my feelings interfere. Sorry I pitched such a fit this afternoon."

Wow, an apology. She must have it worse than I thought. I need to keep tabs on this, but from a distance, if today is an indication.

CHAPTER NINE

My nails are done, now an appointment with my hair lady. For what she charges, I guess she's probably a stylist but that sounds a bit grand.

I hoof it across the street to check in with Nancy. She and her ex were stalwarts in the social mix of Monroe and she got to keep the friends and contacts in the divorce. I'm sure she's going to the DiFazio do and I want to talk about what to wear.

"Pretty much anything," she says, pushing her glasses up. "Jeans are a no-no, and there'll be probably two women who drag their minks out, but most everybody is in cocktail dresses. The guys will wear suits."

"Thanks. I may have something left from the Days of Brandon, but I'm sure everybody's seen it."

"Well, even if you go shopping here in Monroe, everybody will have seen that, too. No sense spending money if that's your concern. I have two fancy dresses and I rotate year to year." She raises her eyebrows and wrinkles her nose, a stink face comment that says, "Who cares?"

I'm cracking up. She's right, these people pretty much lost interest in me when Brandon decamped. Now I'm slightly better than the hired help, a kind of poor relation who they countenance on some occasions.

"Now that that's settled, how goes the research on DiFazio—or is that why you're so worried about what to wear?"

"You can see through me like a clean window. I'm still doing background on how vineyards work. Did you know that appellations are under the ATF?"

Nancy throws up her hands in mock horror. "No! Do you think that's because wine falls under the A in ATF?"

"Oh, stuff it. I know what the end-user is, but that seems like ATF controlling corn or potatoes. Those can turn into alcohol as well."

"It's entirely possible they keep tabs on other crops that are grown solely for alcohol. If you grow table grapes, you don't get an appellation. I'll put this research below your thesis request."

I throw her a salute. "See you at the crush bash," I say and head back to my office. On the short walk, I have a mini-brainstorm. I'm planning to go to the Wine Institute in San Francisco and use that as an excuse to spend a weekend with Phil again. But what if I invite him to Monroe and take him as a date to the end-of-harvest party?

Phil is the art critic for the San Francisco *Times* and he's had a twenty-year career as a journalist. He may be writing criticism now, but he cut his teeth as a general assignment reporter at a couple of L.A. papers and we worked together briefly at the San Fernando Valley daily. An interest beyond being co-workers glimmered until Brandon showed up like a tornado, swept me up to Monroe and dumped me.

Now Phil and I have an occasional weekend. We're careful about making assumptions and there's no talk of permanency, but we enjoy each other.

He'll also add a note of mystery. He's a Québécois, totally bilingual, good-looking and metrosexual. He should have most of the women panting and the men glowering, not a bad combination. Caught off their guard, some of the DiFazio crowd may reveal more information to him then they would to me.

An amoeba-like group is pulsing in front of my office door as I come in. It sorts itself out and I see that Steve has a question, Sandy wants to talk about page one and Gwen is patiently waiting. A "Yes, follow-up on the school board story," to Steve, "Yes, leave a small hole for Angel's follow-up, we'll know when Clarice gets in," to Sandy and "Come on in," to Gwen.

Gwen's been tracking down the levee wine cellar rumor and it turns out not to be a rumor. "You know that fancy subdivision that backs up to the levee by Miner's Slough? It's in the county, the levee belongs to a reclamation district, so nobody was watching too closely. It's true, one of the homeowners dug into the levee and put in a wine cellar. Didn't punch all the way through the levee, but he was getting some seepage. Yelled at the Reclamation District and they came, jerked the cellar out and charged the homeowner for the levee repairs." She has a big grin. "Boy, was he pissed. Wouldn't talk to me on the record."

"Do you think that's a story?"

She's shaking her head. "Not that, alone, but there are a few other wackos in the area. The folks who bought in that subdivision were told the water table there was high, but it didn't sink in. Two of them put in those nice, in-ground fiberglass pools? The ones already shaped? Well, remember the rainy winter we had a couple of years ago? The owners were warned never to drain the pools but one of them did. Trying to "winterize" it. There was so much rain the water table rose, and the pool did too. Popped right out of the ground. Those guys couldn't find anyone to sue. I'm going to work on a story about the pitfalls of living along the levees, both the possible dangers from the water and probable dangers from your neighbors."

She's having a hard time keeping a straight face. "I wanted

to tell all of them that if they had to have a one-acre back yard, they should have bought in the foothills, not in the flood plain."

I OK the story and we both shake our heads. It's good that there are enough people around to keep life interesting and keep our pages filled.

I'm carefully composing an email to Phil when Clarice pokes her head around the jamb. "Not anything new on Angel. The sheriff has sent all the grape knives and machetes they could find to the state forensic lab for blood testing. This isn't a popular move during harvest. The camp manager is buying new ones and the field crews are worried the cost is coming out of their paychecks."

Labor unrest on top of the other ills latching on to the DiFazios? This vintage better be a good one with the grapes bringing high prices, or they won't be making much money this year.

Clarice goes back to the phone to make routine cop calls, hoping to scare up at least a few briefs, and I send Sandy a note to plug the page one hole with a wire story about the wrangling over the state budget. In the flush old days, maybe five years ago, we used to share a pool reporter in Sacramento who covered state stories. A few of the smaller papers in the area went together on the salary and office expenses, and everybody had a first-hand account of business in Sacramento. Now, unless it's a story with a big impact on Monroe, we make do with wire service stories. It's a new game.

I wrap up my Phil email by inviting him to Monroe next weekend for a party. I can't promise him a lot of excitement, but there may be some big food-and-wine honchos mingling with the locals. And I'm planning on taking him to brunch at the Ryde Island Inn, a Delta hotel converted from one of its incarnations as a speakeasy.

There may be ghosts.

CHAPTER TEN

I manage to get home before seven on Friday night. Phil is coming and I'm planning dinner at home—salmon, cheese soufflé, mixed green salad and I'm putting my bets on dessert. I'm making zabaglione, one of those desserts that go together fast but taste like you've slaved all day—my favorite recipes.

It's good I got home early. I'm setting the table when Mac sets up a barking frenzy, telling me that the doorbell rang. "I know, I know, I did hear it."

I'm talking to Mac when I open the door and Phil snickers. "I didn't know you carry on conversations with your dog." He has a big grin and leans in to give me a quick kiss.

By the time I untangle from Mac and Phil and his overnight things, a timer is going off in the kitchen. "Let me get that and I'll show you where the bedroom is," I say as Phil heads for the stairs.

"Don't bother," he throws at me, halfway up the stairs. "This is a foraging expedition to see if I blazed the trail correctly."

The last time Phil was here, we were coming back from an interesting and painful weekend at an old hotel in Marshalltown. He made sure I was comfortably in bed before he headed home to the Bay Area, but didn't stay.

I smile to myself. Phil is resourceful and I can't think he's ever had too much trouble finding women's bedrooms.

Dinner goes off without a problem and the zabaglione is the hit I hoped for. "I didn't know you're such a good cook, Amy. A woman of many talents. And I remember one of them." He cocks his head at me. "So, tell me what you're after with this wine business."

I almost choke on a sip of Port. Here I am thinking double entendre and Phil is all business. "Hmmm, you've heard of the DiFazios, right?"

"Yep, and I did a tad of checking. Not the Mondavis or the Gallos, not so much winemakers as grape growers. But they sell to many of the premium wineries here and in the Napa and Sonoma areas. Good grapes you can use as a base for some of the varietals. Why are you interested in them?"

I do a brief recap of the recent DiFazio troubles. "Clarice is covering all the happenings, and is hot on the murders. Nothing gets that girl going like a little mayhem and some bodies. I'm more interested in why."

"Why what?"

"Why are the DiFazios being singled out? Is there something in their past? Or something they're doing now? Who are their enemies? They've been around this area for almost a hundred and fifty years. That's plenty long enough to engender a lot of anger, bitterness, jealousy and hurt feelings."

Phil's shaking his head. "Have you considered plain old coincidence? If it's some historical secret, why is it coming out now?"

"I don't know. That's why I'm looking. Maybe something is happening that's forcing all this to light."

"I'd think you're dreaming, but I know you tracked down the Senator's past faster than the cops." Phil is referring to the story behind Robert Calvert's theft of a priceless daVinci drawing during WWII. "I'm thinking this searching is behind the invitation for this weekend get-away. Or is it really my witty conversation and buffed body?"

He's wiggling his eyebrows a la Groucho Marx and I'm giggling. "It's both, all, of the package," I say. "Where else can I find someone who knows about the business, has the instincts of Nero Wolfe and isn't afraid to show a girl a good time?"

It's the last that seems to seal the deal. He leans over and gently pulls my chin toward him. This time it's not a perfunctory welcome kiss, it's an "I-remember-and-I-want-you-again" version and it works. I wrap my arms around his neck, lean into the kiss and the electricity begins to spark down my nerve endings to my toes. I can feel the shivers run up my back. I need to get this man up to my bedroom.

I'm up and have coffee made when he comes downstairs the next morning, his hair still damp from the shower. "I thought we'd have coffee by the pool," I say. "It's still warm enough."

He gives me a kiss. "It's plenty warm. San Francisco is chillier in the mornings, so this feels good."

We gather things up and head into the backyard, giving Mac a half-treat. He's thrilled to have a guy around who can throw his ball faster and further than I can, but he also hasn't had his morning walk.

"Are you hungry? I have prosciutto and melon and I'm making a frittata."

Phil nods as he pitches Mac's ball so hard it bounces against the fence. "Sounds good. What are the plans for today?"

"Not a whole lot. We need to be at the club by six for cocktails. I thought I'd take you on a quick tour of a couple of vineyards and introduce you to Nancy, so you'll know at least one person besides me there tonight."

The temperature stays pleasant so I put the top down on my Miata. A slight breeze kicks up by the river where DiFazio's camp for the Govicche vineyard is, and Nancy serves wine coolers on her deck.

As I'd hoped they might, Phil and Nancy hit it off. They both love bizarre and offbeat facts, both love digging in history and both have warped—my word, they think they're hilarious—senses of humor.

We've left enough time in the afternoon for a rest, which turns into great sex, before we shower and get ready for the harvest bash.

The DiFazios always rent Monroe's fanciest (of two) country club for their annual crush party. Valet parkers whisk my car away and we walk up the path that's draped with grape vines and Japanese lanterns.

Inside, the grape theme continues. Vines heavy with grapes hang from the walls, old presses, half-barrels filled with ice chilling Champagne and soft drinks and wine racks are arranged around the dance floor. We pick up Nancy, find our table and begin to mingle.

I know quite a few of the people from my Brandon Days, so say hello, give air kisses and introduce Phil as we wend our way through the crowd. As I hoped, a slight silence follows us. The Monroe crowd is assessing whether I should be dating (shades of tarnishing Brandon's memory) and where I found someone. Unsaid, but I feel the tension, are their questions. "Who is he?" "Where did she meet him?" "From San Francisco? I didn't think she knew anyone there." And from the women, "How'd she find anyone that sophisticated and good-looking?"

When we get to the DiFazios, Carmine is standing, leaning on a cane, while Jules brings people over. It's not unlike an audience with the Pope, or maybe a godfather. I say hello to Jules and Carmine, introduce Phil and we get shunted off to another group where, I'm amazed, Phil knows people.

It's three folks from the Wine Institute in the city and they're chatting with an ad executive who handles one of the most prestigious wineries in the Napa Valley. Whoa, these are heavy hitters indeed for Monroe.

It's Phil's turn to introduce me but we're interrupted by the dinner announcement. When we're seated, I whisper, "How do you know these people?"

Phil gives me an enigmatic smile. "Do you think that money and wine people are separate from the arty crowd? I may cover fine arts, but I do a share of performing arts as well, and did some stories when the Mondavi and Gallo Centers were going up."

That makes sense. Phil's background as a general assignment reporter before taking on the art critic job means he covered a wide variety of stories, and construction of the Mondavi Center for the Performing Arts on the U.C. Davis campus and the Gallo Center in downtown Modesto are just the most recent arts venues paid for by grapes.

We're talking big money here. And Phil and I have one more item on our agenda tomorrow beside brunch.

CHAPTER ELEVEN

After dinner, we make the rounds again and this time he introduces me to the people he knows. I take cards from the Wine Institute contingent and tell them I'd like to come for a visit. We agree to check schedules this coming week and then Phil steers me toward a man talking with the DiFazios.

"Amy, this is Paul Nuncio. His family had vineyards in the Folsom area of Sacramento County in the late 19th century. They were among the first grape growers in this area."

How does Phil know these people? This is my backyard and I've never heard of the Nuncio family or vineyards in Folsom. I can see hours with Nancy coming up.

"It's so nice t meet you," I say as I shake Paul Nuncio's hand. "Do you still farm in this area?" As a fact-finding sortie, it's pretty weak. I should know all the local ag people.

"No, no, we sold out at the beginning of Prohibition." He's in his late 50s and looks like he spends his days behind a desk, not on a tractor. "We went into other crops, mainly orchards, and then began developing our land when Sacramento started to grow. Now, we're mostly developers and into commercial real estate. How do you and Phil know each other?"

"I'm the managing editor of the Monroe *Press* and Phil and I worked together on the San Fernando Valley paper. Are you interested in newspapers?"

I don't think this is a funny question, but Nuncio laughs, a little too hard I think. "No, I don't know the first thing about them. Phil and I are in a wine group in San Francisco. Even though we don't have vineyards any more, I like to keep up with the industry. If my family had known what liquid gold was in those old vines, we may never have gone into development."

Hmmm. It seems Phil has interests I don't know about. Not surprising since we have better than a ten-year gap. Nuncio moves off, I feel a hand on my shoulder and turn to find John Nesman, the Monroe Chamber of Commerce CEO.

"Hi Amy, are you going to do a story on this?" Nesman knows better, but it's a subtle little dig that's intended to nail me in my place.

I give him a bland smile and introduce Phil, which is probably the real reason Nesman slithered by.

A band begins, playing Big Band and early rock. As the dance floor fills up, Phil takes my hand and leads me out for a slow dance. I've always had a theory that men who can dance are comfortable enough with their bodies to be good lovers, and in Phil's case, it's the reverse. He's a warm, caring, sensual lover and his dance floor moves are five stars as well. I close my eyes and feel a slow flush rising. It might be the wine I've drunk, but it's more likely the prospects of later that are making me tingle.

We head out as the party winds down—it's not late, but there's no late life in Monroe. Mac greets us and I can see he's restraining himself from jumping up in his usual "You're here! It's been days!" welcome home routine. He gets let out and fresh water and Phil and I have a nightcap. I'm eyeing the stairs to my bedroom but there are some questions. This is a mixed business and pleasure weekend.

I kick off my shoes and curl up at one end of the couch,

Phil drapes his jacket and tie over a chair, rolls up his sleeves and takes the other end. I guess it's our long friendship that lets us stay away from the randy teen stuff.

"I'm surprised every time we get together. You have some weird encyclopedic knowledge of people and things. I knew you liked wine, but I didn't know you were part of a group. That sounds so formal. Is it like those French groups, with sashes and ribbons and little silver tasting cups?"

He's just taken a sip of brandy and when it hits the back of his nose as he tries to stifle a laugh, his eyes begin to water. "Where do you come up with these things? You're making me sound like I live in a 19th century novel. Of course not."

A cough, a deep breath. "We're just a bunch of guys who like wine. We get together every month, put some money in a pot and invite a wine expert to bring some wine and talk about it. We're supposed to sip, swirl and spit it out but a lot of it gets swallowed. We rotate who's the designated driver."

"Is that where you met those people we saw tonight?"

"Some of them. I met Paul Nuncio in L.A. He had a partner who was making a name for himself in the art gallery world. Did assemblage pieces."

"Where does Paul live? I assumed here."

Phil nods. "He moved back to this area when his partner died. AIDS. It hit Paul hard. He's still on the fringes of the gallery world and when I moved to San Francisco, he introduced me to the guys in his wine group."

I've learned over the years that so many of those things that look like odd pairings or cobbled-together mysteries are simple once you know all the facts. It's this knowledge that I try to get my reporters to grasp. Sure, there are some conspiracies, and some murders go stone cold, and some public officials are on the take, but look for the simplest solution and it's right most of the time.

"I didn't realize I was asking an expert when I invited you over. Can I pick your brain? I don't want this town to start on the conspiracy rag over what's been happening with the

DiFazios."

"I figured you'd have a few levels behind your invitation and that's fine. I'm glad to help and it would be easier if you'd tell me what you're looking for."

I stare into my brandy. Maybe if I look long enough, it would clear into a crystal ball and I'd see a path to take. "That's part of the problem. Clarice and I are just flailing around at ideas. She's pushing the sheriff's department hard, thinking they're covering something up and I'm thinking there are some basic facts we're missing. She's best at the who, what, where and I get stuck at the why. I have this itchy feeling that Prohibition figures into this somehow. I know that's a little off the wall but I'd feel better if I knew all the history."

Phil is edging down the couch toward me. "I'll do what I can with that. Talking to Paul will get a good background on the early history. He knows the DiFazios and some of the other families. Probably the Gallos and Mondavis as well, although the Nuncios were out of grapes early on."

He's close enough now that I lean on his shoulder. "Thanks. Whatever this is, if there is a why, background will help." I turn my head into his chest and inhale his unique Phil-scent of clean, expensive cotton, cologne and just plain old pheromones. It calms me, makes me feel secure and starts some kind of small purr.

He strokes my head and pulls my face up.

"Let's leave history lessons until the morning." He grins and leans in to kiss me and as his tongue finds its way into my mouth, the purr catches on in earnest.

It's all I can do to lock the doors and turn out the lights before we race up the stairs.

CHAPTER TWELVE

This morning is another glorious early fall day with just a hint of briskness. The air still has traces of lazy summer but there's the promise of tang coming. We have coffee before we pack up and head for the Delta.

We drive both our cars to the small Delta town of Walnut Grove, drop his and then I drive to Locke, a historic Chinese town below the level of the levees they worked on. Locke was built about 1915 on ag land the Chinese leased from a local rancher named George Locke. The Chinese Exclusion Act of 1913 made it illegal for Chinese to own land in California and Locke was one of the only Chinese-built and occupied rural towns in the United States.

The Chinese had a long and varied history in this part of the state. Thousands came for the gold, more thousands came for the early construction projects. They helped build the Central Pacific railroad across the Sierra Nevada, the massive levees that hold the Sacramento River in its banks and the Delta wouldn't be what we know today without their efforts.

I could see Phil adding to his encyclopedia, taking in the leaning buildings, the gambling hall and the art galleries that were the leading edge of gentrification. We head across the river. I'm not a nervous driver but I take care on these two-lane winding levee roads. There are no barriers or shoulders, and it's a straight drop to the river on one side and a more gradual drop to fields, homes and orchards on the other. Every year a few cars get pulled out of the river after their drivers failed to make a turn or drove as though it was a freeway.

"I'm coming back to explore this in my car." Phil drives a vintage Porsche and thinks in another life he was on the Grand Prix circuit. Traffic in San Francisco and the Bay Area doesn't give him enough thrill.

I smile over at him. "We'll take some small roads after brunch. It's hard to get lost because eventually most of the roads wind back to the river."

Around a bend and the Ryde Hotel looms on our left. Built in the late 1920s, it's rumored to have been a speakeasy, a bordello and just a get-away spot for notables who didn't want to be noticed. It's Palm Beach pink with a small garden fronting the road and lower floors opening onto the back gardens below the levee.

"It's reminiscent of the Mediterranean," Phil says, eyeing the umbrella tables. "Inside or out?"

I want to soak up the last bits of warmth, plus we'll have more privacy under the umbrellas so we stake a claim with the hostess. Once we settle in and mark out territory with keys, sunglasses, phones, we both start, "I've been thinking..." There's that silence while each of us waits for the other, then "You, first" in unison.

Phil grins and I wave my hands around until he finally says, "Well, I have been thinking..." then he pauses for me to interrupt and goes on when he sees me quiet. "This DeFazio business, I'd look at the history in this area if I were you. An awful lot began or ended with Prohibition."

"I agree. I know that the DiFazios bought out the Govicches in 1921 when they couldn't transition to table grapes and make a living. DiFazios had enough diversification that they stayed afloat. Both Carmine and Jules Difazio studied the market and got into varietals early. They've been growing premium grapes for years now. Maybe one of the Govicches thought they got rooked on the sale. Like Paul was saying last night, the Nuncios got out of the grape-growing and into the land business and they're worth a fortune today."

"Where are the Govicches today?" Phil asks as he catches the server's eye for more wine.

"One branch moved to the Bay Area, I think they own an Italian deli in the East Bay. Others went to the Napa Valley. They're still working in the industry, but for some of the boutique wineries. And a few stayed around Monroe, doing custom farming now and some of the smaller growers contract with them."

Phil looks stumped. "You've been out of the city for too long. What's custom farming?"

"Hmmm, you move to the country and learn something! Custom farming is when you contract with somebody who has the equipment and labor to do crop production. The agreements vary. Some parts of the country, the owner buys all the seed and chemicals, pays the custom farmer a lump sum for the production work and keeps all the crop money. Around here, it's more like the farmer gets a lump sum plus some percentage of the profits. That way, the small vineyard owner doesn't need to buy tractors, irrigation equipment, harvesting machines or hire labor. He contracts with a custom farmer, everything's done, it's still his vineyard with bragging rights and he's paid after harvest."

"Good lord." Phil's eyes are round. "It sounds a lot like sharecropping. Is this only here?"

"No, no, it's all over the country. I think a lot of the Midwest is farmed like this. Unless you have big acreage, it doesn't pay to sink your money into machinery. I can't imagine what one of those big harvesters costs. It's not too far different from the old time threshing crews that used to follow the harvest. They were day laborers, but this way the owner knows that he has his crop worked for the full year."

"Ha, I bet the guys in the wine group don't know about this." Phil's gloating over a new encyclopedia entry. "Do the Govicches custom farm for the DiFazios? I'd think that would rile them, working the same land and vineyards they use to own."

"I doubt it. The DiFazios have plenty of land in vines and even keep a small full-time crew on the payroll. They hire labor during the thinning and the harvest. They've amortized their equipment out years ago and the cost of anything new is spread across all their properties. But the Govicches could still be smarting over what they probably thought of as a forced sale."

Phil's nodding. "Yep. They had no way of knowing that Prohibition was a lost cause and would be repealed. And then, those who could stay with alcohol production were in the catbird seat. Vines aren't an overnight crop...it takes years for them to produce well."

"I'm no expert, but I am learning some things. I know there are some vineyards around Monroe where the vines are more than a century old. Those are the gnarled plants that get head trimmed every year. The newer vines are on wire...those are neat rows you see where the vines are trained to grow upward, not outward. They're easier and cheaper to harvest."

Shadows are starting to lengthen toward the river and we know our time is short. We've stayed so long that we're cutting into the hotel's early dinner service. The staff is way too polite to give us the stink-eye, but they'd like to close this umbrella and move indoors.

Before I take him back to his car, I drive down some of the small roads that intersect and connect all the areas that are now islands. This used to be a huge coastal marsh but the levee system has turned it into sloughs, tributaries and cuts of water, leaving islands of incredibly rich soil. Some of the islands are privately owned and farmed and have no public access and others are wild, with massive oaks meeting overhead on a one-lane road. It's eerie as the sun is sinking, leaving long shadows.

At his car, Phil wraps his arms around me. "This has been a great weekend. Thanks for inviting me. I'm glad I could introduce you to Paul. I'll keep in touch with him and let you know if anything comes up." And his mouth curves into a wicked grin. "Something always comes up when I'm with you."

I grin back. "And it's not wasted. I'd hate to have to choose between your body and your brain. When I get a date set with the Wine Institute guys, I'll let you know. Maybe I can combine business with pleasure. Thank you for coming over."

We hold each other for a moment, then he kisses me goodbye and heads his car toward the freeway and west. I head for the freeway and south, sorry to have the weekend end, but excited about researching.

Whatever is happening to the DiFazios—coincidence, conspiracy or premeditation—may have it's roots back deeper than some of it's head-trimmed grape vines.

CHAPTER THIRTEEN

"OK, it's time we talked to the Sheriff."

Clarice is at my office door and the wash of euphoria from my weekend is popped, faster than a soap bubble around cactus.

"Hi, Clar. Would you care to let me in on your conversation?"

The blond jolts to a stop in front of my desk and her eyes finally focus. "I think the Sheriff is giving us the run-around and it's because of politics."

"That's a bit cryptic. What're you talking about?"

She peevishly brushes stray hair out of her eyes. "Sheriff Dodson is stonewalling me on Angel's murder. I know they must have found something, but I can't get a word out of him."

I notice that she's using Jim Dodson's title and not just calling him Jim. At this point, I don't know whether my admonition caught or she's just steamed at him, but I'm glad to hear her use his title.

"Why do you think he's keeping us, you, in the dark?"

She gives me a look like I'm a brick shy of a load. "Politics."

"What about politics?"

"You know his current term is up in two years and if he wants to stay on, he's gonna have to be elected. Running a race costs a lot of money. He doesn't have any. Well, any of his own. He has to raise it. The DiFazios have a lot of money and clout in this county. Jim Dodson can't afford to lose their support, ergo he's stonewalling on the investigation."

As fascinating as it is to watch her mind weave some suppositions and a few facts into a full-blown conspiracy, I need to stop this before anyone gets wind of it.

"Where'd you come up with that load of bushwa, Clarice?"

"There are some guys at the labor camp talking about it. And I've done some background interviews with guys who hang around the bars by the railroad tracks. Some of them were Angel's regular clients and they're pissed that she got killed and no one's doing anything about it."

Part of what Clarice says makes sense. She did a feature on Angel.

Angel was a hooker, but before she was Angel, she was a popular college student who'd graduated from Monroe High School. She was close to graduating from college with a degree in business when she hooked up with a high-functioning dealer on campus. She didn't do the street drugs and stayed miles away from meth, but cocaine and heroin put her into a place where she could still manage a daily life.

Eventually she figured out that she wasn't going to be able to continue her habit with what she'd earn as a entry-level manager, so she turned to a commodity she knew would sell. The dealer was in the picture, but Angel hadn't studied business in vain. He wasn't her pimp, she was a sole proprietor and their relationship was strictly as buyer and seller.

She made enough to rent a small apartment in a seedy part of town where she entertained her clients. A few times a year she'd be gone for a week or so.

It wasn't in her feature story, but Clarice heard a rumor

she'd go to visit her family and stay until they tried an intervention. She'd also visit the labor camp to pick up a little extra from the crews working the harvest.

Clarice looks at me. "It wasn't a glamorous life but she said she was content. She had a lot of friends in the fringe of the working class and these are the people who want to see her murderer caught and punished."

"We can go talk to Sheriff Dodson, but before we do," I go over and close my door, "I need to know where things stand with you and Dodson."

I hit some mark with that. Clarice has red creeping up from her chest to her eyebrows.

"That's pretty personal, Amy. I don't think it's any of your business."

"You're right, your personal business is off limits, but you made it a legitimate topic when you started seeing him. Now your personal life is part of our business relationship with law enforcement. I have no right or interest in the details, but I do need to know if your relationship has any bearing on where you're going with this story. I'm not making any phone calls until I know there's no personal angle to this."

The red is ebbing. She shrugs her shoulders, admitting I have a right to ask this. "I can promise you, there's no personal angle here. Jim and I are friends who have an occasional date, usually lunch or dinner. I don't know if I'd tell you anything beyond that. We're not like you and Vinnie."

That's a low jab, but I choose to ignore it as I dial Dodson's private line. His secretary picks up and I ask her for an appointment with him.

"I can get you in for a few minutes at three," she says.

"Thanks, I'll see you then."

"Will it just be you?"

Ah, she's clever, or Dodson has trained her well. "No, Clarice Stamms, our police reporter, will be with me." I'm charitable and give him the benefit of wanting to know how many people he'll have to face.

Clarice starts to head back to her desk, but at least throws me a "Thanks, Amy," over her shoulder as she bulls through the door. In the constant game of who's up, she and the other staff know I ultimately have the power cards, but small victories count in the pecking order of the newsroom and I can see Roberts flinch when he hears her voice.

Ah, well, he's constantly digging his own grave, a spoonful at a time.

With a small slice of time, I hit the search engines, looking for any DiFazio, Nuncio or Giovecchi hits. There are several thousand, but not much information I didn't already have. I can't find much on Natoma, except the name seems to have morphed into Natomas, a huge area of housing developments north of Sacramento. It was built in the last 10 years or so on flood plain ag land amid dire warnings that the levees could be breached.

As usual, I'm caught up in tracing research when Clarice taps on the door and points at her watch. I nod, close Google and grab my purse.

We walk the few short blocks to the Sheriff's Department and come through the door of Dodson's outer office just at three. Clarice may have a loose concept of time about some things, primarily deadlines, but she doesn't miss a second where law enforcement is concerned.

Dodson's secretary nods at us, just a recognition that we're here and on time, buzzes him and he opens his door.

I hear Clarice suck in her breath.

CHAPTER FOURTEEN

Jim Dodson is easy on the eyes.
When I first met him in Marshalltown, he was the new sheriff in town. He'd arrived in San Juan County from L.A., where he'd been on a fast career path to a Deputy in homicide, the high visibility and cream in most law enforcement agencies. And there were plenty of murders to investigate. The pace burnt him out and be began looking for a quieter, smaller department.

San Juan County was just a little too quiet, so when the Madison County job came open mid-term, due to the previous Sheriff's heart attack, he applied. Madison County seemed just the right size and intensity level and Dodson is growing into the job, with rumors flying about his candidacy in the next election. Clarice's informants aren't the only ones wondering.

Whether or not he's a candidate, he's conscious of the rumors. He dressed casually but well in Marshalltown, but now he's wearing a dress shirt with French cuffs and his suit jacket hangs on a coat rack. A few gray hairs are sprinkled among the dark ones and he has slight wrinkles at the sides of his brown eyes.

I smile at him, sensing the wrinkles are laugh rather than worry lines. He knew Vinnie's story, but we never bring it up.

"Amy, it's good to see you." His hand is warm and comforting. It's no wonder Clarice gets breathless around him. Her face sports a pink wash when he takes her hand to shake and says, "Clarice, how have you been?"

"I'm fine," she manages to get out.

"What do you two want to talk about today? I'm jumping to the conclusion that it might be Angel."

"I think it's Angel," I say, gesturing to Clarice, "But Clarice is the one who called this meeting."

I can see Clarice struggling to get her blush under control and her business face on. "I've been hearing a lot of chat that the Sheriff's department is stonewalling on the investigation." She roars into business mode. "The word among Angel's friends is that the DiFazios have agreed to bankroll your election if your office stalls the homicide work."

Now it's Dodson's turn to get pink, but his is irritation. "That's ridiculous. You know me better than that. I've assigned two of my best guys to Angel. I haven't been here long, but I know she was a well-known town character and liked by a certain contingent."

I break in. "We're not saying you've done anything to slow things down. We're just the messenger this time, passing along information Clarice hears on the street."

He's mollified at this. "You're right. I'm hearing some of the same rumors. As the new guy in town, I'm learning who to listen to and who to blow off. There are at least three cliques in the department and so far I'm listening to each of them. The one that's easiest to work with are the guys who liked Jackson, the old sheriff, and find it hard to switch loyalties. These are solid cops and will back me if I decide to run and they see I'm not making huge changes.

"Then there's the group who didn't like Jackson. They're harder because they had a candidate of their own picked out. He may put together a campaign. And the third are the chronic malcontents. They'll complain no matter who the sheriff is and are doing their best to lie low until retirement."

Dodson's right. He's walked into the two sides of a new job. There are the ones who say, "We've never done things like that," against the others who say, "We've always done things that way." Both can be deadly.

"I haven't made up my mind about running, but it's tempting to think the DiFazios would bankroll me. They could almost buy an election here. But no, they haven't offered and I haven't asked."

I watch tension slowly draining out of Clarice. "But why aren't you telling me...uh, us, what you've found out? You took the farm tools for blood testing right in the middle of harvest and the guys are having to break in new hand tools and they haven't been told if any blood was found."

"Sure, blood was found. On most of them. These are sharp cutters and clippers and trimmers and there's bound to be blood on them. These guys, even when they're wearing gloves, cut themselves. The problem isn't finding the blood, it's finding out whose blood it is. Despite what you see on TV, you know that DNA testing takes more than a few hours. The one thing we have going for us is that DiFazio checks out tools to each worker for him to use for the season. What we're looking for is a tool that has DNA from different people. And anything with Angel's DNA."

"What if nothing shows up?" Clarice is following along but wants to get to the next step.

Dodson smiles. "There's always the possibility that the murder weapon, or weapons, isn't a farm tool. It could be a personal knife or machete that's two feet deep in river mud by now. We've sent autopsy pictures to the tool examiners at the state crime lab to narrow down the choice."

"When do you expect to have something?"

"I have no idea. This is the state lab. We're not the first priority. We may be so far down the list it might be weeks. No matter when it is, this isn't information I'm going to give you.

You'll have to find it out in court during the trial of whoever we arrest."

Clarice is aware she's pushed the sheriff just a tad too far. "I know that I'm not going to get private information, but can you let me know when you find the murder weapon?"

"If we do, I can confirm what kind of tool it was, yes."

I'm getting tired of this technical seesaw. "When I talked to you last, you said all the problems the DeFazios were having were just coincidence. Do you still think this?"

He sits back in his chair and crosses him arms. Classic "I'm holding it in" posture.

"We believe the truck crash was just an accident."

Clarice is on this evasion in a heartbeat. "Then you're saying the three murders are linked?"

"Until we have more information, I can't tell you that." He turns to me. "If you can treat this as only off the record background..." He trails off, waiting for me to hush Clarice, which I do with a look.

"We're working on the theory that the three murders are related. It may be by the same person, or it may be for the same reason, it's way too early to tell, but there's a strong indication that something's not right at the DeFazio Vineyards."

Ohhhh, Clarice's eyebrows are up to her hairline and her mouth is opening and closing. I know I have a frown wrinkle between my eyebrows.

We came on a fishing expedition, looking for possible election irregularities and a sheriff on the take. Instead, we may have found a serial killer linked to one of the county's wealthiest families.

I need to kick my research into high gear—and call in some help.

CHAPTER FIFTEEN

I look at her. She looks at me. I begin.

"This is going to be tricky. I want you to keep on the murders themselves. Even though Dodson was giving us some deep background, there's a lot that nobody knows yet."

We need to spend some time thinking this through and Clarice needs to temper her usual enthusiasm for head-on confrontation.

"Lunch?"

She nods. Finding a neutral spot to talk trumps the possible animosity of the other staff for spending time with "my favorite". She may be, but I try hard to knit the staff together into a team. No one can put out a daily paper by oneself, although a couple of them would love to try.

I pick a deli that has outdoor tables. Usually I prefer them but today I don't want our meeting to be open to the public. There's a small table at the back and we settle in.

Now it's Clarice's turn. "For starters, they're going to have to announce the murders are connected. Some of that hinges on what the forensics turns up. What if the same weapon wasn't used in them? With all the sharp things lying around during harvest, it's possible the guy used a different knife or machete on each of them."

I look at her. "You're right. There's a lot riding on the autopsies. The forensic tool examiner should sort that out soon."

"And if I'm on the murders, what are *you* doing?"

Fair question. I don't want to step all over her territory, but the itch from adrenaline is scooting along my nerve networks.

"I've started on some history research. Phil and I agreed that Prohibition might be the catalyst that set the DiFazios in motion."

"You and Phil? Why's he involved...other than..." She slows when she catches my look. "Oh."

"He was here this last weekend."

"And are things moving merrily along?"

"Too many questions. I won't pry with the sheriff, you don't pry with Phil. Let's just say both of us are mixing business with pleasure. And on a business front, he's been helpful already."

She narrows her eyes, pulling a thought from the back of her brain. "That's right! You guys went to the DiFazio harvest party! What did you find out?"

"You mean outside of the body in the corner?"

"Yeah, right." She stops for a second, suddenly wondering if I'm serious.

I crumple my sandwich wrapper. "It turns out that Phil is a member of a wine group in the city and he's known Paul Nuncio for years."

"Who's Paul Nuncio?"

I run down the story and the connections and Clarice is following. "So you think that this Nuncio family has some connection with what's happening now? That's a thin thread."

"I don't know if there's a connection. I'm more interested in the history of the big grape growing families around here. We tend to forget what an impact Prohibition had on them. The DiFazios bought out the Govecches...maybe there are others and maybe they feel cheated when they look at vineyards now."

Clarice is nodding but she's not buying it. "Two field workers and a hooker? What possible connection could they have to some maybe shady deal ninety years ago?"

"It's only one thread I'm going to follow. If these murders are tied together, there's a motive. Someone did something to someone else. Maybe these victims were blackmailing somebody."

She snorts her iced tea out her nose and it's a bit before she recovers from her coughing fit. "Amy, you accuse me of conspiracy theories. What in hell could these three possibly find to blackmail any of the DiFazios over?"

Putting it in that light, it does seem I'm headed down the UFO path. "Did I say they were blackmailing the DiFazios? It could be anyone. At this point the suspects could fill a phone book. If I'm going to find out why or how these are linked, I have to start somewhere and the dust of history at least seems safe.

"I've talked to Nancy a bit and she says I need to go talk to the wine librarian at U.C. Davis. Phil also introduced me to some guys from the Wine Institute and I'm going to San Francisco maybe this Friday to chat with them."

"This Friday? Is there a reason to go on a Friday?" She taps her forefinger on her lip and sniffs, as though she's remembering a scent. "Oh yes, that's the day before the weekend. Have you booked a room?"

She's fast enough that she dodges the wad of trash I throw.

I head over to the library as Clarice goes to the Monroe Police Department. If she can't get an immediate story from Sheriff Dodson, she'll try and scare up some crime briefs from the city cops, who sometimes get short shrift from her now that Jim Dodson's in town.

The Sheriff's Department is the lead agency in what one of my copy editors calls the Vineyard Murders—nice and catchy for headlines—because the site is in the county. The DiFazios also own the last small vineyard in the city, the one that's slated for extinction if the mega-church gets approved. Having Jim Dodson on the case isn't hurting Clarice's feelings.

I hesitate at Nancy's office door, afraid I'm taking advantage of our friendship, but she waves me in and says, "Where have you been hiding him?"

"Why? Are you interested?"

She cackles. "I could certainly be interested in that. How long have you known him? And you gave him up for Brandon? Girl, you have serious mush for brains!"

I have to agree with her, but at the time, choosing Brandon seemed more sensible than getting involved with a co-worker. I tell her the story, only leaving out a few parts, and she's nodding with approval.

"It's good you managed to get your head screwed on the right way. You and Phil complement each other in all the ways that Brandon missed. Sure, I'd take him but you deserve him. How'd the rest of the weekend go?"

She may be angling for some *details*, but I tell her about the trip to the Delta and our conversation about history.

"What can you tell me about the Nuncios?" I pull out a notebook and pen.

"You haven't overstayed your welcome here, but you've tapped out my expertise. You said the Nuncios had a vineyard near the Natoma, by Folsom? That's Sacramento County and we don't have that. I could try an interlibrary loan, but most places won't let their local history reference documents out of the building. I'll tell you again, head west."

West. West is the U.C. Davis library, and further west is the Wine Institute and Phil. The setting sun beckons.

CHAPTER SIXTEEN

School is back in session at the U.C. in Davis and the streets are jammed with traffic—about eighty percent of it bicycles. .

The forty-minute drive takes me past dairies, fields, orchards and vineyards, a microcosm of ag wealth. This University of California campus is known as the Aggies, a nod to the past when ag and veterinary departments were the campus' claims. Now, the vet school is nationally-known, the viticulture is studied across the world and the campus has almost 30,000 students, pursuing law, medicine, biology, literature, social sciences, ag sciences and everything else.

The small city has tree-lined streets, coffee shops, ethnic restaurants and shops, with a slow, unhurried feel. And like any campus, it's a hike from the parking lot to the library. The day is warm. I suddenly realize that I'll never pass for a student again. Not only are my clothes—a burnt-orange slim skirt, layered tees, Cole-Haan flats and a Coach bag—way de trop for a student, I'm moving like I'm being chased by time. The students, in shorts, ragged jeans, tees and flip-flops, move at a leisurely pace, caught up in swirls and eddies of groups, chatting about...who knows?

My focus isn't on the day or the weather, it's wrestling with how I want to start my research. It's a toss-up whether to begin with county history or vineyards and grapes so I opt for the land itself.

The student clerk at the reference desk asks for my UC ID. "Are you looking for class material?"

I smile. Maybe she thinks I'm a teacher. "No, just doing some research," and I pull out my press credentials.

This is enough to get me into the stacks and she points the way to the Sacramento and Yolo county archives.

Some of this I know. During the early gold rush years, the land along the American River, upriver from Sacramento, was planted in orchards and market crops that helped feed the growing cities of Sacramento and San Francisco, as well as miners and the foothill towns that sprang up.

Then I run across the first grape reference. By 1863, a vineyardist named B. N. Bugbey was marketing grapes and raisins in Sacramento. In 1865, his Natoma Vineyards produced 10,000 gallons of wine, 1,000 gallons of brandy and 25,000 pounds of raisins.

I sneeze. Not at the amount of wine but from the fine paper dust in the stacks. I'm glad I didn't wear white for this expedition.

Bugbey filed for bankruptcy in 1877 and in 1881 the Natoma Water and Mining Company planted a two-thousand acre vineyard. It was billed as the "largest in the world" until Leland Stanford planted his "Vina" in Tehama County— 3,575 acres of grape vines.

This is astounding. I know California grapes and wines have a long history but I never considered the volume. As interesting as this is, it's not until I find a five-hundred acre vineyard owned by Mario Nuncio that I hit pay dirt. The vineyard sold grapes to wineries around the area for more that fifty years until Prohibition cut the profits out from underneath them. Following the family, I find they developed several tracts on the outskirts of Sacramento and owned commercial buildings in Sacramento, Fair Oaks and Folsom. The last reference to the family in the valley is in the 1960s when Paul's parents moved to San Francisco.

Straightforward. Paul Nuncio is what he seems to be—a comfortably well-off man whose family succeeded by buying California land. I don't find any hint of scandal or of forced sale.

I check my phone for messages and see it's mid-afternoon.

I've spent too many hours out of the office and all I've come up with is some ancient history. On the drive home, I'm turning the rocks over in my brain to see what's underneath. Maybe following the land won't pan out. What if I follow the grapes?

I never paid much attention to what kinds of grapes were and are being grown, except that Jules DiFazio had been instrumental in getting an appellation for Monroe, making his grapes more valuable. And I know his family took an early lead in growing some premium varietals, but I don't know what those are.

What I've found out today is the shallowness of my knowledge. I need to do enough research to figure out the questions I want to ask. I have grapes, gold, miners, railroads, Stanford University, the Women's Christian Temperance Union and $150 bottles of wine swimming around behind my eyes when I come to with a jolt. I'm driving across the Delta and missed the turn-off for the shortcut to Monroe.

As I told Phil, it's hard to get lost out here. It's flat, and the views go for miles. Over the past 150 years, this area has been farmed intensively and where there are farms, there are roads, most of which are named for the towns they travel to. And the road builders wasted as little land as possible, with roads following section markers, meaning abrupt ninety-degree turns.

Once I hit the Monroe-Marshalltown Road my mind freewheels again. Why do I get involved in these hunts? Finding out why people die isn't part of my job description.

Clarice does a stellar job of reporting all the aspects of any death and sticks to the investigation like a limpet until someone is caught, charged and convicted. Many times the "why" doesn't get answered, but the cops and courts don't always care.

When I was a cops reporter, my interests were in the three C's too. I loved the evidence-gathering and forensics and kept a tally of my guesses about the perps. I was right about sixty percent of the time—probably the same as any reader following the case. I've changed, though. Some of it may be that I'm older and I've seen a lot more, some because I'm now angrier at murder, and mostly because I now understand how little I understand about human nature.

A younger me just accepted that there were bad people in the world and they'd lash out. Poor anger control issues, some thrill-seeking, some abuse in their background. These causes are still active, but the experience with Brandon opened my eyes to evil behavior. I gave up my ordered life to shape a new one built around him, thinking he'd see and understand that I was changing for him. Nope, Brandon only saw those actions that directly affected him and had no comprehension anyone else might feel differently. I caught him once flipping through our wedding album, only stopping at those pictures with him in them.

He didn't deliberately set out to cause pain. If his actions had unintended consequences, oh well, that wasn't his problem. AB, After Brandon, I wasn't so gullible about promises made, but my trust in myself and my judgments was shaken. I'm a cynic now and wary of everyone, which makes me need to dig until I find out the "why". There've been a couple of instances where the "why" is because the victim was selling drugs on the wrong street corner, a lousy reason for losing your life, but the vic was cutting into the murderer's profits. Greed is certainly one of the seven deadly sins, especially in today's world.

It's really the great adrenaline rush that comes when I've

put together the puzzle that I'm after. Do I want to share it? Not really. Do I share it? Yes, I do. Clarice is even more of an adrenaline junkie than I am and we both love that "Ah ha" moment when all of our ideas and all of our digging turns out right.

The Bluetooth in my ear buzzes and Clarice's voice is with me.

"Were you picking up some ESP vibe? I was just thinking of you," I say.

She laughs. "No, I'm wondering when and if you're coming back to the office. I've written some briefs and the tox report came back on the driver in the DiFazio truck crash. No substances. The lab did find a tire that was slashed and they're checking it against the grape knives they picked up at the camp, but nothing definite yet."

"And you want me back, why?"

"Well, I want you to read my stories so I can get outta here. I'm having dinner with The Sheriff."

She might as well have air quotes around that. "I'll be there in about fifteen, Clar. I wouldn't want to hold you up."

"OK," she says, oblivious to any sarcasm I may have used.

She's such a cat person.

CHAPTER SEVENTEEN

Daylight's waning when I get home. We're headed into the time of year when I get up in the dark and get home in the dark, with most of the daylight glimpsed out of windows.

Mac is happy to see me and settles for the backyard until his after-dinner walk. He only feels cheated during the winter, when his nightly walk is in the dark. He can't tell time—Lord know I've tried to teach him—but knows enough that when it gets dark and I'm not home yet, dinner's late. A big no-no.

I change into some drawstring pants and a tee. As I'm headed for the kitchen, I notice the light flashing on my home phone. I seldom get messages at home, most people call my cell, so I put it down to a robo sales call and hit the delete button, but stop it suddenly. It's a message from my daughter, Heather.

This isn't good news. Heather knows my cell number and knows my schedule. For her to leave a message is way out of character. Dreading the worst, I listen. "Hi Mother..." uh oh, she only uses Mother when she's trying to wheedle, "I...uh...need to talk to you. I'll be in all evening. Talk to you later."

Cryptic. And not cheery news. I dial her number in Santa

Barbara and get one of her roommates who yells, "Heather, your mom's on the phone" in a voice that could call the cows home. Heather yells back, "I'll take it in here..." wherever here is. Ominous. She doesn't want to talk to me in front of her roommates.

"Hi honey, what's up?" I keep my voice light and noncommittal until I can suss out the lay of the land.

"Hi mom, thanks for calling. I need to talk to you about school."

We're back to "mom", in a younger voice. "What about school? Please don't tell me you've flunked something." Bad mom reaction.

"Why do you always assume that I've done something wrong?"

"Fair enough, it was only meant as a joke, I know you just started this semester. In fact, I was on the Davis campus today."

"What were you doing in Davis?"

"Just doing some research in the library for a story we're working on. But this wasn't what you wanted to talk about."

"No. I just found out some news that you won't be happy about. Crap, *I'm* not happy about it."

"And this would be...?"

"I can't graduate this year."

I realize I've been gritting my teeth. My jaw is stiff enough that I have to move it around before I can ask, "Why?"

"It's a combination of things."

"And those are..." I'm sure this conversation is as awkward for Heather as it is for me.

"Remember when I changed my major a couple of years ago?"

She'd started UC Santa Barbara as a Social Science major, planning to eventually get a MSW and work with children. During a session with an academic counselor she learned what the pay scales were for an entry-level MSW and began looking around at other options. She didn't want to get rich, but she wanted to make enough to live comfortably, so she hit on nursing. She'd still be able to work with children if she went into pediatrics and the pay scales were considerably higher. She interviewed a Pediatric Intensive Care Unit nurse, found that she made close to $100,000 and switched majors the next day.

The fly in this ointment was that Heather was sketchy in the math and science department, so she spent a year picking up the basics for anatomy and microbiology and now the nursing program was so jammed that she'd have to wait for at least a year to get the final classes.

This isn't good news. Her college fund stretched to cover most of the five years she's spent already. Anything extra has to be loans or my mortgage payment.

"There is some good news. I can only take six of the units that I need this semester, so I can work a lot more. I'm going to ask my manager for another fifteen hours a week and that should be enough to cover my living expenses."

I'm surprised. This is an unexpected reaction and my heart swells. It's such a grown-up way to handle bad news and my eyes get a tad moist.

"Honey, it sounds as though you've got this all figured out. Did you just call me to announce it?"

There's a short silence. "Nooo. I'm trying to be careful, but I think I'm going to be a little short each month. Could you send me some?"

"How much is 'some'?"

"Maybe a couple of hundred? And, oh, maybe pay my car insurance?"

The sound of the other shoe dropping echoes through my head. I can pay her insurance in a lump sum and scrape up the other easily, just cut down on IRA contributions. Who knows, if she makes a ton of money, maybe it's still paying toward my own retirement.

"I can manage that. How's your roommate situation?" A few months ago her two roommates had a huge blowup and one of them moved out, leaving Heather and Jen with a big rent payment. They'd searched until they found another young woman who seemed compatible.

"It's much better. Madison is quiet, she studies a lot and she's neat. Pitches in on chores. Doesn't even mind going grocery shopping."

Knowing that Heather and her previous roomies would eat dry cereal before going to the store, this warms me. "Are you guys hanging out together?"

"Not a lot. She's been here four years and has a bunch of friends she hangs with already. The ones we've met seem pretty OK. Mostly they're fresh air and magazines and a couple of Lit'n'Lang."

I have to translate. Madison's friends are majoring in business and literature, liberal arts. "You might get some help with papers, then."

Heather sighs. "I just have nursing classes and rotating internships left over the next year. I don't think I'll be writing many papers. It's enough that Madison pays her rent on time and is willing to go shopping. I don't think we'll be BFFs."

I laugh. "Those are good traits. Send me your insurance bill and let me know when you need some money. I love you and miss you. You can call even though you don't need anything, you know."

Now she laughs. "I know. And I love you, too. By the way, how's that guy in San Francisco?"

She's becoming an adult. I'm a little sad.

CHAPTER EIGHTEEN

When I open my email this morning, I have a lunch invitation from the Grands.

They invite me once or twice a year, and I always attend. I haven't joined any groups or clubs in Monroe. My reasoning is that I don't want to appear biased in any way. I've seen too many times when a group wants you to slant a story or do a feature, trading on your acquaintanceship.

The Grands are different. They're a group of women who met one another some thirty years ago in the League of Women Voters. Most of them went on to successfully run for office and now they're in their 70s and 80s and retired. They're getting physically frail—two are in wheelchairs, one uses a cane and we talk in loud voices—but they're as sharp and involved as they ever were and their lunches are a smorgasbord of local and regional topics. They invite me when they want to float trial balloons about issues.

Today, the issues run from falling—some are developing balance problems—to a quick discussion of hearings aids and water diversion from the Delta. One of the new local assembly members is thinking about a run for the state senate, because with term limits, he'll be out of office in six years when the senate seat is up again. He's starting to look for endorsements and one of the Grands has been asked.

They're a loose-knit group, now primarily long-term friends, and they're all independent. They'll usually share information about endorsement requests, petitions, speaking, public hearings or media appearances. They've been networking since before the word became a verb.

As the meal winds down, one of them, ever so subtly, introduces the topic du jour, the coming election which will include the Sheriff.

Janet, a retired county supervisor, says, "It looks like a short ballot this time."

"So far not a laundry list of propositions." This from Sandra, a former mayor.

I'm waiting. These women don't indulge in idle chatter when politics are involved.

Janet turns to me. "Didn't you have some dealings with Jim Dodson when he was in San Juan County?"

Ah ha. "Yes. The Sheriff was the lead investigator in the Calvert murders. We found him easy to work with."

"Are you working with him and his office now, here in Monroe County?"

"The Sheriff's office is the lead in the investigation of the murders at the DiFazio vineyard, yes."

Now Susan, a previous city council member, says "Is he planning to run for office?"

"I don't know. Has anyone asked him about it?"

There's a spate of conversation that boils down to a rumor that one of the top deputies in the department administration has asked a couple of the Grands, absent today, for endorsements. They won't be so formal as to ask the candidates to come for interviews, but Dodson is still an unknown and they'd like some feedback.

This is a tad touchy because ultimately we, the Monroe *Press*, will be making formal endorsements for all the races and I don't want the Grands to think we've chosen a candidate yet.

"I can tell you my impression of Jim Dodson, but it's sketchy. I don't know him well and only worked with him on a couple of cases. For the record, though, he did know my late husband, Vincent Hobbes, in Southern California."

Several of the heads around the tale nod. "Did they work together?" Janet leans forward to pick up her coffee cup.

"No. My husband was a city cop. He was killed in a high speed chase that the Sheriff's department was following. I didn't meet Jim Dodson until he was in Marshalltown."

"Why did he leave L.A.?" She sets the cup down. It rattles on the saucer and I realize her age is showing. Her hands shake slightly.

"He told me it was getting too hectic...too much work, too many killings. He wanted a slower pace. You should probably ask him, though. I don't feel comfortable guessing about any of his personal information. I just don't know him that well."

"You said he was easy to work with." This from Susan.

"Yes. He would keep us apprised on the case and call us with information. He also asked if we'd send our stories on to the larger papers, hoping that might stir up more leads."

"Did he ever ask you for anything you couldn't provide?" Mary, a former mayor and attorney in the D.A.'s office is toying with her napkin.

"I'm not sure I know what you mean."

Her eyes bore into me. "Did he ever ask to see a reporter's notes?"

That startles me. Asking for a reporter's notes is not done. Communication with sources is privileged under the First Amendment and California's shield laws. As an attorney, Mary knows this, then I realize this is a test, both for me and for Dodson. I smile.

"No, he knows where the barrier is between the press and law enforcement. We both understand how much information can be passed back and forth. He won't jeopardize the ultimate prosecution and we won't help them put the case together."

Mary sits back. "Have you heard anything about who's paying for his possible campaign? Does he have a committee yet?"

That's a pointed question. I'd have thought this was information they already knew, so the chances that DiFazio is pumping money into coffers is moot.

"I haven't heard anything. It's too early for an announcement even for an exploratory committee. Have you heard anything?"

Mary shakes her head, leans over to pick up her cane and lunch is over.

It's too bad, because I like these women and I don't see much of them other than these lunches. I know that Gwen and Sally see them occasionally at various meetings around town. I mentally remind myself to call one or two of them and just have coffee together.

I don't tell anyone about the Dodson questions. The Grands were just gathering information, off the record and for background, which I understand. What may happen in the way of endorsements or backing will play out in the months before the election.

Dodson hasn't announced, but I secretly hope he will run. I'm fond of him. I trust him and I think he'll take the department into the future in terms of new forensic science and community policing techniques. The Sheriffs and the candidates historically have come up through the ranks which means what was good twenty years ago is likely the way it still happens. No whiff of scandal, no accusations of incompetence, just a "business as usual" mind-set.

We can all use a little change to keep us on our toes.

CHAPTER NINETEEN

As I get in the car, a text message from Clarice. "Better get back. You have a visitor."

"Who?" Her next text: "Haven't a clue. Looks pissed."

Great. All the warm feeling from lunch with the Grands evaporates. I hate being screamed at. I hate people who are pissed. I hate people who are pissed at me without even knowing I'm only the messenger. As I get out, I slam the car door, then have to apologize to her. It's certainly not the Miata's fault that somebody's unhappy.

I round the corner and see a man sitting in front of my desk. He's maybe in his early 50s, graying hair, a face that's seen a lot of worry, shirt and tie, no jacket. As I come in he stands, a gesture I don't see much any more. He's a couple of inches shy of six feet and is beginning to slip in the war with gravity.

"I'm Amy Hobbes. How can I help you?" My tone is carefully noncommittal.

He takes my hand in a perfunctory shake. "My name is Samuel Bonham."

I nod. His name tells me nothing.

"My daughter is Jesse Bonham." I nod again. My face must

look quizzical because he adds, "I think you know her better as Angel."

OMG, this is Angel's father!

I sit down, hard. Use a few seconds of putting my purse in a desk drawer to gather myself. Why is Angel's father here? And why is he pissed at me?

"What can I do for you, Mr. Bonham?"

He runs a hand across his hair. I think Clarice read him wrong. He doesn't seem pissed as much as worried sick.

"I know what Angel is...was... My wife and I came to terms with it. My other kids don't have anything to do with her, but Jane and I, her mother, hold...held...out hope that she'd change."

He begins a story that's so personal it'll be painful to hear. "Jesse was our oldest. She was such a leader. She had good grades, lots of friends, was helpful to us, cared for the younger ones—we have another boy and a girl. We don't know what happened at that school. Maybe it was the big city—she went to college in San Francisco—maybe it was the people she started hanging around with. Whatever it was, by the time she graduated, we knew she was hooked on something. It wasn't until a few years later that we learned it was heroin.

"When she moved back to Monroe, we were relieved. Maybe at home, with her family around, she'd be able to kick it. Then we learned that she was a..." He stopped, not able to call his daughter a prostitute.

I waited. He finally said "a woman of the streets. We tried to get her help. We even tried an intervention, but she'd chosen a life that satisfied her." He shook his head at facts beyond his comprehension.

"Jane and I went through counseling and came to understand that it wasn't anything we'd done or didn't do. Jesse was a grown woman and made her own choices, even though we hated them."

It was one thing to talk about the town's best-known hooker but it was another to listen and watch as her father grieved for her.

"I'm sorry for your loss, Mr. Bonham. What do you want from me?"

"I'm not stupid. I know what the facts are. But when you run stories about her being killed at the labor camp..." His eyes are wet. He has to clear his throat before he continues, "When she entertained men at her apartment, we didn't know about it. It wasn't public. But at the labor camp, having sex with all those farm workers, it's so public."

"Mr. Bonham, I'm sorry, but she was a prostitute and she was working at her business when she was killed. We can only tell the facts." I watch him. Is he one of the locals who think farm workers are beneath dignity, people who don't deserve anything from life? Lord knows, they have little enough but is this man ashamed his daughter had been murdered while with some of them?

"It's just that her murder involved so many people. And so many suspects. The Sheriff's office hasn't been very helpful. Every time we call, there's another test they need to do, or more people they need to talk to. They haven't found who killed her or why she was killed. They haven't even found how she was killed.

"They won't release her body to us, so we can at least bury her as part of our family."

Now his eyes overflow and tears trace down his cheeks. "Because they don't know anything, you run stories about the investigation. And every time you run a story, it opens another wound for us. I want them to find the murderer. And I want to watch that man get his just desserts at a trial. And I want that man to suffer the rest of his life, as we're suffering. Please help us. Please make the sheriff's department find her killer."

"Mr. Bonham, I can't 'make' the Sheriff's department do anything. We'd like to see the killer caught as well. Why do you call the murderer 'that man'. Do you know a man did it?"

"No, no, I have no idea who did it. If I did I'd be living at the Sheriff's. She was stabbed and it just seems like a crime a man would commit."

I pick up a pen and begin doodling in my notebook. Is this man wanting us to stop the coverage of his daughter' murder because it's embarrassing to him? Or does he want us to keep writing stories to keep pressure on the department to catch the killer? He's distraught enough that he probably doesn't even know what he wants, besides having the last decade replayed the right way.

"If we continue to keep your daughter's murder in front of the public, we may have a chance of jogging someone to tell what they saw. Or have a new witness come forward. Or have somebody who fishes a machete out of the canal turn it over to the Sheriff. It's painful for you and your family, but in the long run it can help find her killer. Is there any other information you can give us?"

Samuel Bonham sighs and stands up. "No. Just that she was a good girl until she started using that drug. I'd like everybody in Monroe to remember her as she was, not as she ended up."

As he walks out I have a flash. I wave at Clarice to come in.

"That looked like it went well, he didn't seem too pissed. Who is he?"

"He wasn't too pissed, at least not at me. That's Angel's father."

This rocks the blond back. "Angel's father? I didn't know she had one...well, of course she had one, everybody does, but I didn't think about him still living in Monroe." Frown lines are appearing between her eyes. "What did he say?"

What did he say? He told the story that most of us know from the gossip mill but this version is fleshed out. "Don't think so hard, you'll end up with permanent lines. Listen, I have an idea I want to talk over with you."

Now smile lines at the corners of her eyes replace the frown. She's always pleased when I want to work with her on something the other staff doesn't know about.

"Shoot," she says.

CHAPTER TWENTY

"We're not getting much from the Sheriff, but it's probably because they don't have much to give. What if you do a feature on her family? Not like the one we did a few years ago, the 'Day in the Life of a Hooker,' but a look at what murder does to a family. Even if the victim wasn't a sterling character?"

Her eyes squinch up and her nose wrinkles, this time. She doesn't like features, too "touchy-feely." This one might intrigue her. It's a feature tangential to her beloved cops beat, there's murder involved and it may have information for Jim Dodson. I watch the trifecta form behind her eyes.

"What are you wanting to find out? Her family can't have anything to say—her dad came to you for help." A sudden gleam. "Wait a minute, are you asking me to get them off your back?"

She's not completely oblivious and starts back-tracking when she sees the ice in my eyes. "I don't mean you're just making work for me...you're not just hoping for them to go away..." She dribbles off like the end of a flash flood.

"No, Clarice, I see this filling some cracks. Readers like to learn about families coping with stress, the family can give

Angel, or Jesse, a decent farewell and something in Angel's background might turn out to be useful."

Now that she's blown off her initial steam, calculations play across her face. "I could talk to her family, her neighbors, maybe some of her 'clients'. She went to high school here, right? Might be some of her classmates are still around."

I think she's hooked, but I throw out a bit more chum. "We could put together a package, or run it as a serial if we get enough."

Oh boy, now she's flopping on the bottom of the boat. "She was a heroin addict, maybe a sidebar on that intervention stuff that's so big right now. And another one on the drugs available and how they work. I always thought of addicts as drooling fools, just getting it together enough to get their next fix, but Angel managed to have a kind of a life."

She has a far-away look. She's thinking this can be page one for a week or so and give her some great clips.

"Clar, I'm not planning for this to be an ongoing Sunday centerpiece or a prelude to a book..." Oops, now I see her visions of a six-figure advance, a book tour, guest spots on talk TV.

Her eyes focus. "I'm not planning that Amy. It's just there are so many ways to go on this topic. I wonder if there's a group for victims' families here, you know like the National Center for Victims of Crime. I'll need some time for research."

For all that Clarice drives me nuts, she's a solid professional and I know these stories will be fleshed out and well-written. She's already writing the lede as she floats to her desk.

Before I start scanning the budget for local stories, I shoot an email to Phil. I want to talk over some of this with him, not for him to direct me, but to think out loud. Being the boss can get lonely and I need an objective voice. He responds, saying he'll call me at home tonight. I have a little pulse of pleasure behind my ribcage for the afternoon and manage to get home, walk Mac, and pour a glass of wine when the phone rings. Whoever invented caller ID has my undying gratitude.

"So what's up?" His voice has an edge of amusement. "Can't manage without me?"

"Right... not! First, are you free next weekend?"

"I could be for the right offer."

"I want to spend some time at the Wine Institute. There's a branch office in Sacramento but the mother ship is on Market at Fremont Street. I know they're a marketing group, but they also lobby on legislation and have big clout with the Ag committees."

"OK, but they're not open on the weekend, are they?"

"Hummm, no. I thought I might come over in the afternoon Friday and meet you somewhere for a drink afterwards."

"You're going to drive all the way over here for a drink, then drive home? What're you after?"

"Well, I was thinking...."

"You're beating around the bush, Amy. What's up?"

I tell him about my conversation with Heather and that my budget's going to be tighter for the next few months. Which means I can't afford many get-away weekends.

He laughs. "That's a shame...I was attracted to you for your money. Well, it's been nice knowing you."

The phone goes dead. That asshole hung up on me!

My cell rings and it's Phil again. "What's going on! Why'd you hang up on me?"

"I didn't hang up. Uh oh, has that guy been impersonating me again?"

"What guy...oh, you idiot."

"I do what I can to leave 'em laughing," he says and now he's laughing. "You sounded so businesslike and rigid talking about Heather that I had to bring it down a notch. We can have weekends together any time you want. All you have to do is let me know. I'd love to have you whenever you can get here. And that certainly goes for next weekend. If you'd like, I can get some of the wine group guys together for dinner Saturday."

"I'd like that," I say and give him a quick rundown of the history I uncovered, then a segue to my meeting with Samuel Bonham.

"Sounds as though he's on the edge. I can't imagine what it would be like to lose a child, even one who's picked a dangerous and different life."

I'm nodding. It's funny how body language works, I know perfectly well he can't see me. "Yep. I've assigned Clarice to do a story, or maybe a series, on living with the grief of having a child murdered. She's off on tangential research."

"She'll do a good job. Send me copies when she files and I'll see if we can run them. She'd get a 'Special to the Times' byline if we do."

Now I have some real bait for the blond. Clarice works hard and I know she's headed out of Monroe to a larger metro daily, but I don't want it to be any time too soon. In a selfish way, I'm privately encouraging the Dodson interest, just another filament in a web to keep her here.

"Thanks, Phil, I know she'll appreciate it."

"By the way, the Sacramento Art Museum is putting together a show of loaned things from the Modern Movement Gallery here in about six months. I'm working on some stories of what this kind of loan entails, everything from curating the show to packing, shipping, showing. I'm planning to be there for the opening and do some interviews with the locals. Maybe you could put me up for a couple of days, payback?"

"You know I will. And bonus points, you already know where the bedroom is."

A tingle of warmth blossoms and moves up the back of my neck.

"See you next weekend." I shiver as I click off.

CHAPTER TWENTY-ONE

Clarice's eyes round and the familiar pink tide washes over her face. "Really? I'd get a 'Special to' byline? That's great, Amy!"

I can tell she's literally tickled pink that Phil would go to bat for her with the San Francisco *Time*s.

"These are going to have to be features with a broad appeal." I need to impress on her that she's writing general interest pieces, cautionary tales that most readers regardless of location can relate to. This means she'll have to do some substantial research, do phone interviews with experts in addiction, heroin use, intervention techniques, and if she can track it down, another family willing to talk about the toll addiction took on their family. The Bonhams will still be the core of the stories but now there's an overreaching story being told.

"Who's gonna cover the cops while I'm working on this?" This is a double-edged question. First, does she have to have some boob making calls to her beloved cops, and second, how much time will she be given to finish up this project.

I have to nip this in the bud. "First, nobody's going to cover the cops except you. And second, you won't get extra time. You'll have to work the project around you usual beat."

"But, Amy..." Now she has a look of stunned disbelief.

"Calm down, Clar, we're going to sit here and work out a timeline. I'll have Steve work with you on covering some of the basic calls. It'll give him some experience with breaking news."

She's nodding. She doesn't know Steve well, but she also hasn't lumped him into the boob-pool in the office. "I'll start with him this afternoon." Ever the eager beaver, Clarice isn't going to waste a minute more than she has to on education.

"Wait a bit. We'll have to work out a timeline for this that you can mesh with your regular stories. I'll talk to Steve this afternoon and you can begin showing him the ropes tomorrow. Now, where's the big calendar?" I keep a wall calendar for vacations, planned absences, contest deadlines and projects in the works. It's not detailed, but it gives me a snapshot of available staff in case something breaks.

We agree that Steve will do basic calls for three days next week while Clarice does phone interviews with people she scares up. By next Friday we'll sift through what she has and outline the articles needed to tell the story. I can help her carve out writing time and we'll start the series with a Sunday package. I know this isn't how the big dailies, the ones that win the Pulitzers, do things, but we don't have the staff or the time to free up a reporter for weeks at a crack to research and write.

She's back at her desk, jotting notes and searching Google. I send an email to Phil about my success with Clarice and tell him as soon as we firm up run dates, I'll let him know.

Now it's my turn to hit the search engines.

For millennia the rivers washed down from the Sierra Nevada and drained into San Francisco Bay through the bathtub plug that's the Delta. That left miles of silty soil and, with a mild climate, it was ideal for growing Mediterranean crops—like grapes. In the nine counties around Sacramento alone, there are two hundred and ten wineries using thirty-four grape varieties.

I can't use this, there's just too much information. I need a primer on what's grown and why. A trip back to Davis, and this time to talk to the viticulture librarian. As a first step, I call the Chamber of Commerce. John Nesman creeps me out with his smarmy personality. He's a toady, but he does know the ins and outs of businesses in Monroe.

"Well, Amy, I didn't think you'd come to me for information, I figured you're too big city now." I can feel the smirk oozing down the phone line. "What can I help you with?"

I'm nervous about giving Nesman a one-up in the favor tussle. "This is just for my own background, John," I begin. "We write a lot about the wine industry and vineyards, I'd like a rundown of the different grapes grown around here. Which have the biggest acreage, which pay the best, just general numbers."

"Hmmmm," I detect a subtle sound of glee in the response. "As for which pay the best, that's a variable. Depends on the weather, the amount harvested, the amount the wineries want, the sugar content, what's gaining or losing in popularity. That can change. And how many acres are planted in any particular grape—that shifts, too."

Is this man capable of giving a straight answer? "I understand that, John. I'm looking for overall trends."

"I always call vineyards and orchards the 'futurist' crops. You have to be in farming for the long haul when you're growing cherries or pears or almonds or grapes. And grapes are the most tenuous. With tree crops, they take a long time to produce, but the variety of pears or cherries stays the same and nuts, well an almond is an almond."

He's showing a slight sense of humor, not something I'd given him credit for, and passing along information I can use. We might reach detente yet.

"Grapes have a popularity factor." His voice drones and I fight a yawn. "If pinots are hot sellers, you can't take a chance and tear out older zinfandels. By the time the newer vines are producing, the wine drinkers may be on to some variety only grown in Chile, so you have to be diversified and keep your eye on the market."

"That's all good information, John, but can you tell me some specifics? Which grape has the biggest acreage?"

"Right now, Zinfandel, Cabernet Sauvignon, Merlot and Chardonnay are the biggest. There are still some old growth Carignans and Petite Sirahs being grown and a few people have put in Syrahs and Viogniers. We'll see how those do."

I'm jotting down grape names. "Who grows what?"

"DiFazio grows all the reds, even the older blending grapes like the Carignans and Petite Sirahs and they have acreage of both old and new Zins. The Hermanns are the whites; they're Chardonnay. The newer ones are the small 50-acre plots—guys who grow for the boutique wineries here and in the Napa area."

It galls me a tad but I say, "Thanks, John, you've been helpful. I needed some overall background before I go and talk to the viticulture librarian at Davis."

There's a sucking sound then a small cough. "Why are you going to Davis?"

"Just trying to get more educated." I laugh, but he doesn't laugh back. There's a flat silence. Over the years I've learned to just let the silence stretch. It's a way to find things out when the other person breaks down and fills the vacuum. I'm beginning to think John didn't read that part of the book.

"I want to look at the history of the grape growers in this part of the state," I finally say. "I discovered that some of the vineyards on the American River go back almost to the gold rush."

"That's true." I hear a small sound, almost a sigh. "We don't have information about any areas other than the Monroe appellation. Is this going into a story?"

"I doubt it. It looks as though I'm staying in Monroe and I want to know as much as I can about my home. Thanks again for all your information."

He hangs up. I swear I heard another click seconds later. Was someone else listening to our conversation?

No, Amy. I mentally slap myself for tipping into the conspiracy zone and make notes for the Wine Institute.

CHAPTER TWENTY-TWO

It always charges me up to be in San Francisco. It's compact, it's busy, people move around with a sense of purpose and now in the early fall, it's summer.

During spring and summer, as the inland valleys heat up, the wind comes through the Golden Gate and up the rivers. San Francisco stays cool—some tourists in shorts call it cold—and foggy and the Delta area is bearable. At the northern and southern ends of the Central Valley, summertime temperatures regularly reach three digits and days of one-hundred-twelve degrees or so aren't uncommon. Now, it's cooling off in the valley and warming up along the coast so I only take a light sweater along for dinners with Phil this weekend.

The Wine Institute is the advocacy and promotion arm for California's wine industry and carries a big legislative clout at the state and federal levels. When I scan the handout the press person gives me, I can see why. With about 3,500 bonded wineries and 4,600 growers, it's a major industry that employs 330,000 people in the state with almost $20 billion in sales across the nation.

I come away with a briefcase full of reports, graphs and

white papers and have a better understanding of the work that's gone into building the California wine image.

Phil's sent me a text to meet him at his house and I fight traffic up to Russian Hill. I'm in luck, I find a parking spot only two blocks away and can easily haul my small bag, purse and bulging briefcase. He must be waiting because my buzz is answered immediately and when I shove open the outer door, he's grinning down the stairwell at me.

"Traffic?"

"Not too bad. It beats sitting on an L.A. freeway at rush hour." I know he understands; we worked together in the San Fernando Valley, where traffic is brutal.

He comes down a flight and takes my briefcase with a grunt. "What'd you do, pack rocks?"

"No, a stop at the Wine Institute. With these pounds of paper, I'm planning to write a master's thesis on California wine."

He looks at me strangely as he holds his apartment door open, and I crack up at his expression.

"Are you kidding?"

"Yep, I'm kidding. The PR person was helpful, but there's so much to go through with all the legislation and statistics, I figured I'd be better off toting this information home. I'm not up against any deadline, not even sure what I'm looking for and have no idea if there're any answers here. At least I can use it to work out my arms."

He grins, drops my briefcase, takes my bag and purse and reaches his arm around to bring me to him for a very satisfactory welcome kiss. When I pull away to catch my breath I get a good look at his working uniform—pressed blue jeans, laundered and starched white shirt, silk tie, now askew and ...bare feet?

"You go to work barefoot?" I'm on the verge of laughing.

"Of course not." He nods at a pair of tasseled Italian loafers kicked off beside the couch. "You caught me before I could change. I can only take so many hours in a starched collar."

"I can understand that. It takes something special to get me into pantyhose any more. But your wine dinner may do it. If I get a chance to grill them, I want to be professional."

He comes back into the living room. He's put my bag in the bedroom and finished stripping off his tie. Now he rolls the sleeves of his shirt up to his forearms and I get a good view of his hands and the long, expressive fingers. I know those fingers can type about 70 words a minute (he told me) and I know some other things they can do as well. I'm impressed, typing well has never been one of my abilities.

"We talked abut getting together for a drink. We're together, would you like a drink?" He's cheery. "We can watch those poor people trying to head home across the bridge," and he waves out his window at traffic crawling east to Oakland, Berkeley, Walnut Creek and beyond. "I'm so glad I'm not part of the bridge and tunnel crowd."

I smile and kick my shoes off as well, curling up in a corner of his couch with my arms around a pillow. "Sure. I'll have white wine if you have any. That seems appropriate after today."

"Of course I have white. Does a Sauvignon Blanc sound good?" He heads into the kitchen and I hear glasses clinking then sounds of something being chopped. He brings the wine, goes back, chops some more and comes back with a plate of bruschetta.

"So tell me, how're the stories on the Bonham family coming? Do you have a schedule yet?"

"No, I gave Clarice a week to begin the research and line them out. We're meeting later for a final sked. I'm planning to run the first one, an overview, next Sunday."

He nods. "When I talked to the features editor about them, he was excited. Especially since they're a run-anytime series. Your schedule is more time-constrained."

I have my conversation with John Nesman sitting in the back of my consciousness. I can't pin it down, but something is unsettling and I test it out on Phil, telling him about Nesman's reaction when I mentioned Davis.

"Are you sure he sounded, what, concerned, worried? He might have just been distracted."

"He might have been. I don't know if he was worried, but the tenor of his voice changed. It sounded like he was, maybe, frightened a little."

"Are you going to let this stop you from going?"

"Lord no, it's a niggling feeling. He always makes my nape hair stand up."

We have another half-hour of business chat...who's been fired, who's been bought out, who's moving on. It's depressing. It used to be we'd talk about who was being hired, who was working on an investigative piece, who might be up for a Pulitzer. And always, circulation figures. Used to be going up, now they're going down. We're both quiet, giving a moment of silence for the death, or at least the terminal illness, of America's newspapers.

Phil and I are glad we still have jobs. Not so long ago, being a journalist was interesting and creative and a solid, honorable career. We're remembering as we watch the lights come up on the Bay Bridge.

"Before we get too dismal, what do you want for dinner?" His voice in the twilight startles me out of my wandering and less-than-happy thoughts. If the Monroe *Press* succumbs, I don't have an exit plan.

We decide on the Ferry Building and taking potluck with whatever looks best or can seat us and end up with a nightcap at a neighborhood bar near Phil's. Once back at his house, I'm yawning and he asks if I want to go to bed or go to sleep. I can't make a decision between those two so he puts my purse and sweater in a chair, walks me to the window, now looking at a necklace of orange strung across the bay, and takes me in his arms.

"It's still your choice," he murmurs as he leans down to kiss me. "I'm just going to tilt the scale a bit."

The scale whips over and I kiss him back, my need for him spreading warmth from my core. Not even a contest, as it turns out.

CHAPTER TWENTY-THREE

Phil's "wine guys" turn out to be eight men ranging in age from about 30 to maybe 85. I recognize Paul and he gives me a hug and a kiss on the cheek. There are five other women, mostly wives, as this morphed into a social gathering. They've reserved a separate room in an Italian restaurant in the Marina and it's clear this group has partied together for several years.

There are whites and reds, six courses and lots of laughter and discussion. One of the men begins a story about a trip to Italy and by the punch line, "I tripped over a vine in the dark," the rest chorused in with "and came home in a cast," followed by gales of laughs and a stern look from his wife.

Phil leans over. "So far, they haven't been able to get me to go on one of their little overseas excursions. I may, though. They're talking about Burgundy, staying in Beaune. That one may be hard to pass up."

I nod. I've certainly heard of Burgundy, although I'm not sure I could place it on a map of France. I idly wonder if my research into vineyards can justify a trip. Naw, not until Heather is established.

After dinner, Paul brings two men, Gus and Walter over. "Amy is doing some research on the history of vineyards and wineries in the Central Valley, around Sacramento," he says. "I've told her some of my family's background." He turns to me, "Both these guys are from German families who settled in Sacramento and San Joaquin counties. Their families were early into wine, The courses of the rivers reminded them of the tributaries of the Rhine. Like mine, they're out of the vineyard business but still have wine in the blood."

Gus is probably the oldest man here, about eighty-five, and Walter runs him a close second. They have old-world mannerisms, despite their ancestors having been in California since 1870 or so. Walter is short and round and looks a little like a German garden gnome while Gus is taller with a patrician air.

"I'm happy to meet you." This is from Gus. "Phil hasn't mentioned a lady friend and we wondered..."

"What Gus is trying to say," from Walter, "is that Phil seems lonely at times. It's nice to see he has friends outside of our group."

I smile at both of them. If only they knew Phil's L.A. background with high-powered, beautiful women. It was enough to daunt me, and even now I wonder if there's someone hanging around the edges.

"I guess I qualify as a lady friend. We've known each other for about twenty years, but were surprised when we both ended up in Northern California. A pleasant surprise. What varieties of grapes did your families grow?"

"My great-grandfather brought over Riesling and Gewurztraminer cuttings and we grew the light Rhine grapes here. They weren't as popular as some of the heartier reds that were produced." Walter points to Gus. "His family planted Chardonnay and some of them are still producing in the old mixed variety vineyards. They usually get bottled these days as California white table wine."

"Do either if you still have vineyards? Most of the old families seem to have sold out."

They nodded and Gus said, "Prohibition was the end for

us. We had fifty years of farming but by then the cities were growing and our land was worth more with houses or stores on it. If only we'd had a crystal ball and seen what wine's doing now... His soft blue eyes grow pensive as he imagines what might have been.

It makes me sad to hear these stories of old families forced out of the farms and careers they loved for such a short-lived thing as Prohibition, but that was then. Clearly it hasn't dampened the interest and love these guys have for grapes and wine, and they all seem to be well-enough off.

I'm feeling pleasantly buzzy when Phil comes over and quietly asks if I want to go. I glance at my watch and am jolted when I see it's almost midnight. I don't have a curfew, I'm not going to turn into Cinderella, but I am suddenly tired. Along with giving up high heels—well, I was wearing a pair tonight, *and* pantyhose—I've given up nights that end up in hangovers the next day.

We say our goodbyes and head out the door. The fog has drifted in while we were eating and drinking and I feel comforted and cozy, wrapped in soft, damp white. Back at Phil's the foghorns are mournful, calling out their different tones and cadences and maybe offering remembrance sonatas for the early sailors who lost their lives coming through the Golden Gate.

Phil lights a fire and pours us each a brandy. The necklace of lights across the bridge takes on a diffused glow and seems to beckon to the east, as though it leads to the gold.

"Did you enjoy tonight? I'm always a bit anxious when I bring someone new, someone I care about, into an established group."

I can feel a question mark wrinkling my eyebrows. Phil? Anxious? Those aren't two words I'd put together. "I had a wonderful time. All the wine guys are interesting, I liked their wives...or girlfriends. I especially enjoyed Walter and Gus. It made me melancholy to talk to those men who were pushed out of what they loved because of Prohibition. Thank you for inviting me." Then I shut up as his words sink in. "Someone I care about," he'd said.

"Gus said it was nice to see you with 'a lady friend.' Does that mean I'm the only woman you've asked to the wine group?" I won't go on a fishing expedition for complements or explanations, but a straight-forward question can't hurt.

He leans over, sets my brandy on a table and strokes my cheek, running one of his lovely, long fingers across my lips. "You're the only one," he says as he folds me into a kiss.

Ashes in the grate are still warm and the smell of last night's fire mingles with a strong scent of coffee as I come out of Phil's bedroom in the morning. It's clear he's an earlier riser than I am. At one time, I may have had a nudge of guilt, but now I bask in having coffee ready.

Except as I follow the coffee aroma into the kitchen, there's no Phil. He isn't in the living room, I know he isn't in the bathroom or bedroom, I check the small brick patio. Has he been abducted? Good lord, I may not have the full brunt of a hang over, but I'm showing the muddle-headed thinking. As I shake my head, the front door opens and he walks in.

With breakfast.

A warm baguette.

Soft cheese.

A melon.

Some prosciutto.

And the Sunday papers.

Heaven.

CHAPTER TWENTY FOUR

The day is cool. We opt for indoor activities and head to the Legion of Honor for a late lunch, a tour of the galleries and the afternoon organ concert. We wrap sweaters and jackets around us and walk across the road to look out at the Marin headlands and the Golden Gate Bridge from the ocean side. Fog wisps through the tops of the bridge towers and the wind picks up, making the stiff eucalyptus leaves chatter.

I shiver, Phil opens his jacket and wraps us together. I lay my head back on his chest, feeling safe, warm and cared for. If I could package this feeling and sell it online, I'd be an internet millionaire, but the realies pull me back.

After two nights of watching the cars headed east on the Bay Bridge, I join the exodus, leaving the sun setting behind me. Clarice has dropped by to feed Mac and walk him, a favor I relish and try not to use too much. He bounds up to me with his usual breathlessness, asking "Where'd you go? I thought you weren't coming back! I haven't eaten in days! There's something I have to check out in the neighborhood, I heard noises!"

I scrub his ears, let him out in the back, fill his almost-full dish—proof that he's transferred some affection to Clarice—

throw on some shorts and a tee and walk him around the neighborhood. He greets everybody, stops at each lawn to check out the recent traffic, hides behind me when the Schnauzers two blocks over bark at him, comes home and with a contented sigh curls up on his dog bed, watching my every move in case I bolt again.

The house feels stuffy and too warm after being closed up all weekend. I take a plate of cheese and crackers—no wine tonight—out by the pool and let the remains of the day's warmth soak into my bones. I'm tired and a little blue, missing Phil already, but I force myself back inside to check email. I don't want to start a Monday playing catch-up.

No crises pop up so I go to bed and dream about necklaces of light.

Monday, when Clarice blows in about noon, she sticks her head in my office and gives me a Groucho leer. "Well?"

"Well, what?"

"Well, did you have a good time?"

"Yes I did. And thanks for looking out for Mac. He tried to tell me that you hadn't fed him, but his dish was almost full."

"That guy! We get along fine when you're away, but I know he misses you."

I smile. It's good to have someone miss me. "What's on tap for you today?" I have the daily budget, a list of stories coming from the reporters, open on my screen and don't see a lot of stories from Clarice.

"I thought I'd take Steve with me to the cops and sheriff. Introduce him around, see if we can pick up any briefs."

This is a good idea. With Clarice, I know she won't let much of the really good stuff on the cops beat get away from her, but having Steve familiar with the routine will free her time to work on the Bonham project.

"One thing I didn't mention is that Phil talked to a couple of editors at the *Times* and they're waiting for your stories. I'd like to send them a budget."

This hits the mark. Clarice's fair skin is rising pink and her grin even wrinkles her eyes. "That's super, Amy. I know we said we'd work out the stories on Friday, but can we do it tomorrow? I want to get started on this."

"Umm, sure, if you think everything's covered."

"I'm not going anywhere," Clarice tenses and she's put on her stubborn face. "If something blows up from the cops or the sheriff I'll be here to cover it."

Placate a bit. I won't treat her with kid gloves, but I don't want any of the staff sensing a tiff between us. Some of them are grand masters at wedging shims into collegial relationships until something gives. Clarice and I are wedded, or at least engaged, in making the *Press* a solid news platform that we can use to leverage our next career moves.

"I'm not suggesting dereliction. Don't overwork or overschedule yourself." Treading the line between an order and a suggestion, a slack-wire balancing act I play with her.

I'm glad Clarice doesn't have long hair, or she'd toss her head so hard she'd give herself whiplash as she stalks to her desk.

Scheduling, scheduling. I'm playing a game of chess with staff members, making sure everything is covered and no one's working overtime, when the phone rings and I see it's a UC Davis number. In fact, it's the Special Collections archivist who wants to set up a meeting between me, him and a specialist in the viticulture collection. He says he has "something you'll want to see".

I count this as serendipity; now I can spend time digging around in their brains for some of the definitive information I need about grapes and winemaking. And this time, I've learned enough to know what questions to ask.

"Yes, I'd like to come over," I tell the archivist. "I can make it this afternoon, if that's convenient."

There's a small silence and I realize I've been put on hold, then he's back. "This afternoon is a little rushed. Can you make it on Wednesday?"

"Wednesday it is. Thanks." I pencil it in my calendar and stare at the wall, making mental notes of what I want to know. A tap on the door brings me back and Clarice is standing there, looking odd. It's not a sheepish look or a stubborn look or a vindictive look, all of which I've seen on her face. If I had to pin a name on it, it's nervous, bordering on scared.

"What's up?"

She waves her hand in circles as she takes the chair in front of my desk. "I don't know, exactly. I'm feeling a little squishy about calling Bonham. I'd like you to call and set things up with him."

This is an admission I never thought I'd hear from Clarice. She usually just bulls her way into meetings, scenes, situations, asking questions like an assault rifle. "I don't mind doing that, but why?"

The blond is quiet for a moment. "Something about this is uncomfortable. It's not just the family of a murder victim, I've done that. It's not just the drugs and the life, though I'm not sure I've ever interviewed a hooker—a least not about *being* a hooker.

"I kinda like the idea of putting her whole story together. Everybody knows that people on the fringe came from somewhere, have some background and family. Maybe it's what Sheriff Dodson said, if these all tie together, do we have a serial killer here?"

She gives a tiny shiver and even I have goose bumps on my arms, thinking there might be a stalker and killer out there. Every journalist knows about the Zodiac killer, the guy who terrorized the Bay Area and taunted the cops through letters he sent to the San Francisco *Chronicle*. Even now, some thirty years later, his killings are still unsolved and the mystery surrounding him is strong enough that it became a Hollywood movie.

"Are you afraid that you may be a target?"

"NO, no, well, I don't know, maybe...I just feel funny." She gives a small smile. "Boy, do I have a way with words!"

I smile back. "You do, Clar, but I also understand those queasy feelings that you can't quite articulate. Sure, I'll call him and set something up. Do you want me to go with you?" This could make her even more uncertain.

She hesitates. "No, I can manage. Even telling you makes me feel better, knowing somebody understands."

I call Samuel Bonham, He's receptive to the idea. "I know you can't make the sheriff do anything, but maybe this coverage will help him out in some way, keep the focus on trying to find her killer."

He agrees to talk to Clarice on Wednesday while I'm at UC Davis.

Our week is filling up, but no action in sight.

CHAPTER TWENTY-FIVE

Davis is humming. The campus is in full swing now. Parking is iffy and I end up in the new structure beyond the Mondavi Center, making my hike to the Shields Library even longer than last time. Now I wear a comfortable pair of flats and cotton slacks with an overshirt, but even with this, I'm sticky from the warmth when I come into the library foyer and head for the elevators.

The viticulture bibliographer, Gustav, is a wealth of knowledge and tidbits. He tells me about a fraud case involving grape growers, brokers and a winery that passed Barbera off as Zinfandel grapes more than twenty years ago. He tells me that Zinfandel is one of the most popular grapes and it's the California state grape. He tells me that some California juice gets shipped elsewhere to be made into wine, including some 80,000 gallons that went to a Long Island winery to ferment and get labeled as their wine, but "made from California grapes."

"I thought that Zinfandel was a newer variety of grape." I say with visions of the white Zin advertisements rife when I was in college.

He shakes his head. "No, it's really quite an old grape. You could buy seedlings from nurseries on the East Coast in the 1820s. It's from Croatia."

Speaking of old grapes, he segues off to the Natoma vineyard and says that they grew a big assortment of grapes, "but they weren't really very good. The land was better suited to orchards than grapes."

When I tell him that the original grower, Bugbey, became known as the Raisin King, he snorts. "Seems like a good use of the grapes!" Gustav's expertise is grapes for winemaking, not land history.

"Why does the ATF oversee vineyards?" Even though I understand the connection between wine and alcohol, I'm still wondering why the California Department of Food and Agriculture isn't the overseer for grape production.

"It doesn't. The state ag inspector's responsible for the vineyards, the grapes, all of the agricultural parts of it. The ATF comes in after the crush, when fermentation starts. And they keep meticulous records. The state ag department doesn't have the money or the staff to watch every vineyard during every harvest. They've put together a loose-leaf notebook of pictures of grape leaves and clusters so they can tell what's being grown when they do spot inspections."

"Wait, wait. Do you mean the only thing they use to tell what grapes are there is to look at the leaves in the notebook?"

Gustav smiles. "Basically," he says. "The leaves and the shape of the clusters. These are pictured in the book."

Through the sudden silence in his cubicle I can hear phones ringing, keys clacking, muted conversations. With all the technology around today, it seems weirdly retro to go around to vineyards with a loose-leaf notebook full of pictures of grape leaves. I don't know what I expected. He sees the puzzled look on my face.

"If we have any reason to, we can do some molecular testing on the berries."

The berries? I'm still puzzled. Like most businesses, wine

has it's own vocabulary.

He looks at me. "The berries are what we call the individual grapes. Berries make up a cluster."

OK, then. I'm not going to ask why they don't call them grapes.

I discover that winemakers will come to the vineyards during the growing season to check on the grapes and run tests for the sugar in them. It's the sugar combined with the yeast during fermentation that determines the alcohol percentage in the finished wine. I also find out that the sediment left from the crush, a combination of seeds, stems, leaves, pebbles, maybe a bird's nest or a couple of small rodents and called pumice, is sold for animal feed or fertilizer. The extra ingredients show up when the vines are mechanically harvested.

The pumice is different from those older vines that are valuable or hand-picked, which is a percentage of DiFazio's crop. It still has seeds, stems and leaves but the field mice and bird's nests aren't included. I wonder about the feasibility of checking each brand of wine I buy for where the winery buys its grapes and how they were picked, but decide to just forget that fact.

He's in the middle if explaining a "label-only" wine maker—someone who rents a larger winery's equipment for crushing, fermenting or bottling their own brand—when his phone rings. It's a short conversation; "Now? Good. We'll be right down."

Once in the Special Collections, I'm introduced to the archivist, Dave. He's knowledgeable and enthusiastic about wine, grapes, the history of this part of the state and probably a wealth of other things, but my time is limited.

He gives the call sheets to a student and back comes a cart with two volumes on it.

One of them is a copy of the ag inspector's notebook, filled with loose-leaf pages of grape and leaf pictures and typed descriptions. It's interesting but what really rocks me back is the second one. It's a casually bound book of thick paper pages, with spidery late-nineteenth century handwriting. The first few pages are alphabetical tabs by grape varieties and the next almost two hundred pages are grape leaves.

Honest to God pressed grape leaves more than one-hundred-fifty years old. It reminds me of the pressed flower books that Victorian ladies put together and I'm stunned.

I look at Gustav. "These are the leaves of all the grape varieties grown in the Natoma vineyard. Sort of an early-day version of the inspector's notebook. Grapes have always been identified by their leaves."

He and Dave carefully flip through some of the pages, all with the same elaborate handwriting, and point out some of the differences to me. I know I miss the subtleties but even my untrained eye can see there's a big difference in size, in how deep the jagged edges go, in how many lobes the leaves have.

It's not DNA testing, but it's stood the test of time for basic identification, much like fingerprinting.

Gustav shows me the pages with Barbera and Zinfandel leaves and they do look identical to me. "This is why the grape brokers could pass the Barberas off. This had to go all the way to molecular testing before the fraud was discovered."

"Is the fraud just because it was a different grape they were selling to the winery?" I'm curious about why this is a big deal.

"No, there's a lot of money involved, too." Gustav runs his hand over his bald head. "The price difference was as much as $1,000 a ton and overall in 2007, there were more than 400,000 tons of Zins harvested and crushed in the state. Even if less than ten percent were some other grape—well, you can do the math. And in the Central Valley, these vines produce up to 12 tons per acre."

I can do the math. And it's an amazing amount of money. I'll have to find out how much acreage the DiFazios have planted in the various varietals, but whatever it is, their Zins are making them money.

Special Collections are in the white glove section so there's not as much dust as the county archives, but a very faint musty smell comes up from the leaves. It's not a grape scent but I can visualize the heat and dust and have a small pang for the vineyard worker given the task of recording all the plantings.

"The Natoma Vineyard didn't last long," Dave says. "They found out early that the bench lands along the American River were better suited to orchards and the Napa, Sonoma and San Joaquin valleys were closer to a Mediterranean climate, so the vineyards moved."

I doubt I'll ever be able to treat a glass of wine with nonchalance again. A little knowledge can be a dangerous thing.

I hike back to the car, get stuck in traffic sludge and come into the office grumpy. My attitude doesn't improve when I spot Clarice pacing in front of my office. She greets me with, "Where have you been? Why didn't you answer your cell?"

My cell is in my hand and I start a snide comment when I realize I turned it off in the library and forgot.

"I've been in Davis. Why the snit and the panic?"

"We need to talk to the Sheriff again. The tox reports came back on the bodies."

CHAPTER TWENTY-SIX

I wave Clarice in my office, dump my purse, cell, keys, sunglasses and plop in my chair. "I'm judging from your behavior that we have a surprise?"

She's in the office too. The pacing has stopped because she's perched on the edge of my desk, but her free foot is swinging like a metronome for a mazurka. It's bouncing so fast she could win a 440-yard dash if the other foot kept up.

"They found traces of heroin."

"Duh, Clarice, Angel was an addict. Of course they'd find heroin."

She gives me a look that could make raisins of the expensive Zins and blows wisps of bangs out of her eyes.

"I'm not talking just about Angel. They found heroin in the field workers, too."

This news startles me. Field workers don't make much money and a big chunk of what they make gets sent back to Mexico for their families. Where were they getting the heroin and how were they paying for it? We seriously need to talk to Jim Dodson and maybe the DiFazio *jefe* as well.

Dodson answers his phone with, "Hi Amy. I wondered how long it would take you to call."

"I guess you know why I'm calling, then. Can Clarice and I come talk to you about the tox screens?"

"Sure, but you'd better hurry. I just got a call from one of the Sacramento TV stations and they're planning to come down. You know, there's still a lot that I won't talk about."

As we walk into the Sheriff's Department, we see a TV van crawl by, looking for a parking spot and a suitable backdrop for the reporter. Jim Dodson stands and we shake hands before he closes his office door. "I'll have to talk to the TV people, but if you have specific questions, we can carve out maybe twenty minutes. And you're welcome to stay for the TV interview."

I'm afraid to look at Clarice, I can feel rising anger boiling off her like steam. She hates broadcast journalists, has no respect for the job they do, calls them "sprayheads", one of the only printable names, and does her best to ignore them. Which is hard to do with their cameras, cables trailing across the floor, lights, mic booms that remind me of Heather's childhood slippers, and their pushiness.

"When did you get the tox reports back?" Clarice is out of the gate and heading for a wild ride.

Dodson knows her and takes it in stride. "We got the results about two hours ago. I pulled a task force together and we'll be working on our strategies this evening."

"A task force? Who's on it?"

Dodson gives her a lazy smile. "I won't tell you names, you know."

"I know, that's hush-hush. At least tell me which agencies."

"There's us, the Monroe police, the Regional Drug Task Force folks, the FBI and the DEA."

The FBI? The DEA? This seems pretty high up the food chain for the murders of two field hands and a hooker. Clarice is right behind me.

"Why are the feds involved? Is this more than local murders?" She's concentrating and making squiggles in her notebook. I think idly that it's a good thing Clarice's notes have never been subpoenaed...no one would be able to read them.

"It's a new protocol we're using," Dodson is patient, but his expression says he's not thrilled at the inclusion of the feds. "We have Mexican nationals, we have drugs in their tox screens, we don't know how these puzzle pieces fit, so now any time we have these incidents in common, we call in all the forces."

"Does this mean you suspect drug smuggling? Are the workers bringing in drugs when they show up for the harvest?" Clarice is all ears and eyes now.

"No...or I don't think so. The more the various agencies pool their information, the clearer we'll be able to see any patterns. At this point it's information sharing only."

I'm aware of bustle in the hallway outside Dodson's office and I try to wrap this up before the TV crew comes in. "Will you keep us informed on the task force and what it's turned up?"

He nods as the PIO opens the door and announces the crew. Clarice and I can't figure out a way to make a graceful exit, so we schooched together next to a bookcase and watch the broadcast reporter go over the same field we just plowed. I'm secretly tickled that they drove all the way from Sacramento to get information one step up from "No comment".

The Sheriff is courteous and wraps it up with, "We'll be calling a press conference in a day or so, as soon as we've compared notes and have a plan. Thanks for coming down."

The crew leaves, Clarice and I exhale and Dodson leans over and asks Clarice, "You're not planning on writing a story, are you?"

"There's not much here, yet. It'll be a short one that you've formed a task force, the feds are here and heroin was found in the tox screens. That's not a surprise to anyone who knew Angel."

"It was common knowledge that she was a user, right? After her body was discovered I went through the *Press'* archives and read the stories you'd run on her background. Seems like a sad life." Dodson is looking at Clarice in an odd way, so I excuse myself and head out to the lobby. It's not long before she shows up, her face warm. I know she hasn't been on a treadmill. I just look at her until she says "What? What?"

"Nothing. You need to change your lipstick if you're going to be that shade of red very often."

She has the grace to smile at my small crack and we walk outside. "He, the Sheriff, Jim, asked me out for a drink, maybe dinner, depending on what time he can get free."

As a woman and a friend, I'm happy for her; as her boss I need to warn her. "Be careful about what you and Dodson talk about. You don't want anything coming back to bite either of you."

The pink deepens, but now it's irritation. "I know, Amy. I can quote chapter and verse of your and Vinnie's relationship. I am careful. Both of us are. He's not naive about the press and I don't want to jeopardize my future. I don't think it's in Monroe."

I touch her shoulder. "OK, Clarice."

I'm tidying stuff up to go home when she sticks her head in my door. "I talked to Bonham today. I'm going to work on the first draft tonight before I make the late cop calls and I'll send you a copy."

"How was it? How was he?" I remember the desolate man in my office a few days ago. I don't think even catching his daughter's killer will pave over much of the hole in his heart.

She shakes her head. "It was OK. No, it was rough. I feel for that man, that family. Read it and see what you think."

CHAPTER TWENTY-SEVEN

After dinner, after a walk, after an hour or so of mindless TV, I log on, check my email and find Clarice's story draft.

It's excellent. She's pulled her story-telling skills together with clear, lucid writing and has the beginnings of an award-winning piece.

"Samuel Bonham is gray. He seems to fade into the wallpaper in his Monroe living room. Maybe his blood isn't circulating. Maybe his heart doesn't have the strength any more.

"Since Bonham was told of his daughter's murder, his world is black and white.

"Samuel Bonham's daughter was Jesse Bonham, known better as Angel, Monroe's best known prostitute. Her body was found recently at the labor camp for the DiFazio vineyard."

Clarice has gone on to describe Jesse's growing up in Monroe, her relationships with her parents and siblings, her accolades at Monroe High School. She was voted "The Most Fun" and her picture was scattered throughout her senior yearbook. She went to San Francisco State University and did well her first year, then seemed to get lost in the 30,000 student campus.

Her dad talked about feeling helpless as Jesse floundered. She had a hard time making friends. Her grades slipped. She badgered him to move off campus and he reluctantly agreed to give her the money to share a house with some other students, friends he didn't know. She only came home for special occasions and stayed in the city during winter break. She got a job at a coffee shop that morphed into cocktail waitressing when she turned twenty-one and didn't come home during the summers.

I have to stop reading this. It's the story of a lot of college kids, but it so easily could be Heather's story as well.

How do people, parents, watch their children grow up and move out into their own lives? What heartbreak happens when a mom or dad sees a grown child make calamitous decisions? How hard is it to sit back and know disaster is coming...and also know that your kids have to face it themselves?

Samuel Bonham has been incredibly open with Clarice and she treats his story with compassion.

He didn't know how Jesse first found heroin. She did tell him that the drug erased her fears, fears he never knew she had. That "Most Fun" girl had been hiding deep terrors of never measuring up, always falling short of perfection.

"Her mother and I didn't see any of this when Jesse was in school. Maybe we didn't want to. Our daughter was the popular one, the one who went to all the parties, who had friends, was always going somewhere. She'd tear through the house like wind on the way to another fun thing."

Her dad said they were relieved when Jesse managed to graduate from San Francisco State. "It took her six years, but we were so proud of her. What we didn't know was what it had cost her." They found later that by graduation Jesse was hooked, shooting heroin daily.

"She didn't tell us when she moved home. I got a call from a friend who spotted her down by the bus station. He said she looked bad and asked if she'd been ill."

This is first draft that Clarice has filed. I edit it and send it back with a note that the San Francisco *Times* will love it.

A pall hangs over me. I have to send Heather a quick "I love you and am thinking of you" text before I wrap it up and head to bed.

The morning TV news runs the story, with shots of Sheriff Dodson and a picture of Angel taken from her high school yearbook. There's not much news in the story and certainly no more than we had last night but they have a banner, "Drug Smuggling in Monroe Woman's Death?" About the only thing they didn't do was call her a hooker in the banner. My heart goes out again to Samuel Bonham. I hope he'll see this in the light of finding Angel's killer.

Clarice is heading out for the DiFazio labor camp to talk to the field boss. I'm dying to know what's going on but don't want to step on her toes and tag along. I call Jim Dodson and ask if I can come over and meet the DEA guys. Are they really building a case for an international smuggling ring right here in Monroe?

Dodson is a tad reticent about my meeting the lead DEA guy, Aaron Skies. He turns out to be a smallish man, maybe thirty-five, with thinning fly-away blond hair that does a halo effect against the light. I had a mental picture of a narc as a beefy guy, dark and bristling with tattoos—similar to my vision of drug dealers. As usual, my assumptions aren't right. Drug dealers can look like Angel and DEA agents can be less than six feet tall.

Skies' handshake isn't the least wimpy and he drills into me with icy pale blue eyes. "Hello, Ms. Hobbes. I hope you know that meeting with journalists isn't usual. You did get a good recommendation from Sheriff Dodson and I did a background on your deceased husband. What can I tell you?"

The first thing is, you did a BACKGROUD on Vinnie? Who died and made you God? Not a great way to start a conversation.

"I know you're part of the task force that Sheriff Dodson pulled together, looking at the tox screens from the vineyard murder victims. Is this a protocol step in deaths involving heroin?"

"No, of course not." Skies' tone is as frosty as his eyes.

"Then why are you involved?"

Dodson clears his throat and I take a mental step back. This guy Skies is making my hackles stand up, but if I lose my professionalism, I've lost the information war.

"I think what Amy means is that it's unusual for the DEA, or the FBI for that matter, to be involved in a purely local murder investigation."

He shifts his attention to me. "I called the federal agencies to come down and help us. The combination of the drugs and alien workers looked like there might be a connection to some of the smuggling rings."

I can have a perfectly civil conversation with Dodson. "I thought most of the drugs coming across the border were marijuana and cocaine, not heroin. I'd always wondered if smuggling marijuana into California was like carrying coals to Newcastle, given what a cash crop that is here."

Skies doesn't thaw at my lame attempt at humor but I do get a slight smile out of Dodson. "The specific drug isn't what worries us. It's how the victims got their hands on the heroin. We know that Angel was an addict, but was her supplier tied up with the labor camp?"

I think to myself that Clarice may be getting the answer to this. "Didn't you search the camp? I'd have thought when you brought all the knives and machetes for examination that you'd turn up any drugs."

"We weren't looking for drugs, we were looking for weapons. If a dealer is out there, he would have been pretty stupid to keep any after there'd been three murders. He'd know the police would be all over it."

Skies has watched through slitted eyes and says, "You haven't answered my question, Ms. Hobbes. What can I help you with?"

I choose words and thoughts carefully. This isn't a brain-picking expedition like Dodson and I engage in. "I'm confused. Two field workers were found stabbed. Then a local woman was found in the labor camp, also stabbed. Now the tox reports come back saying all three of them had heroin in their systems. If drugs were at the camp, I'd think marijuana would be more likely than heroin. And if there's smuggling involved, I'm assuming you're looking at Mexico, which isn't a big poppy growing area. So why would you or", I look at Dodson, "any law enforcement be interested in looking as a drug connection?"

A smirk comes and goes and it's a second before Skies says, "We've developed some additional information we're looking at."

Ah, the old string-a-bunch-of-words-together and see if it flies technique. This has been a fruitless hunting trip and from now on I'll just confine my intimate chats to Jim Dodson. My blood pressure will much appreciate it.

CHAPTER TWENTY-EIGHT

By the time Clarice and I have a chance to compare notes some of my pique at Skies has evaporated. I tell myself and Clar that he's just doing his job, it's nothing personal and the blond slaps a hand over her mouth so her guffaw isn't heard across the newsroom.

"Right, and I'm the tooth fairy! Those guys are just too slick. It's their job to keep us in the dark as much as possible."

"Whatever, we're going to have to talk to him again at some point. I'm just trying to keep it as civil as possible. How'd you do with the boss?"

She shakes her head. "He didn't come right out and tell me that there's a group of men coming up from Mexico every year to work the harvest who bring along a few kilos."

"No kidding. I wonder why not?"

"I don't know. I'm so straight-looking and persuasive that I'd think he'd confess to me."

She looks a bit frazzled. The daytime temps are cooling with the early fall weather, but it can still spike an Indian summer day and this is one. She's been outside at the camp and the heat and dust from trucks and harvesting equipment have taken a toll. A sheen of dust sticks to the perspiration on her arms and there's enough ground mica in it that she glimmers.

"He admits that many of the guys in the crews smoke a little weed from time to time, but he's adamant that it's never during work hours. And he claims that he's never heard of any of the guys doing heroin. It's just too expensive."

"What about Angel being out there? Wasn't she too expensive, too?"

"She had a sort of sliding fee scale. Several guys on the DiFazio crew were regulars. Either they were permanent employees, trimming, cultivating, irrigating during the winter and then thinning and harvesting, or they came back year after year. The employees were clientele year-round so they always had a small discount and usually visited her in town.

"During harvest, though, it was harder to get into town. They were so busy, working seven days a week, that she'd go out there every other week or so for a night. She still kept her regular rates low because she knew that even if they were working overtime, they needed to send the money home."

My tongue is between my teeth and I'm trying not to draw blood from biting it too hard. "Clarice, this is beginning to sound like one of the worst old clichés...the hooker with a heart of gold."

"No, she was just a working girl who wanted to keep her steady customers."

"And was the *jefe* one of them?"

She has a sly smile. "He denied it, at first. Because he's been with DiFazio so long, and worked his way up, his family is here. They live in a regular house on the edge of the camp. He finally admitted he paid Angel for oral sex every so often but begged me not to put it in the paper. I can't figure out how it would fit, anyway, so he thinks I'm doing him a favor."

Clarice is good at using sources and this little omission may come in handy, but sometimes I wish she wouldn't tell me.

"So, what take does he have on her murder? He knew her and both the workers. Is there a tie?"

"According to him, the only tie is that they'd both paid Angel for sex at times. He claims he didn't see her at the camp the night she was killed. He was with his wife and kids at a son's soccer game. The first he knew of it was when the Sheriff's people showed up after her body was found."

"Something's just not adding up. The DEA isn't talking—of course—the FBI hasn't even called a press conference, Sheriff Dodson is hanging back, letting the feds take the lead ...do you think the drugs are mixed in with this?"

I don't for a minute feel guilty about trying to think our way through this without the cops involved. We'd never write or print a story with our opinion about a crime, or what we may uncover. The simple truth is that we will only run what we've gotten from the public record, or in some cases a trusted anonymous source, and that's because of potential libel. We're not big enough to have a team of attorneys—shoot, *one* attorney—but do have an attorney on retainer for those few times we need to have him vet a story.

Talking it over, though, gives both Clarice and me a chance to try out theories which in turn can lead to those questions we need to ask.

"What if we're missing a big piece? What if Angel's dealer was at the labor camp? What if it's someone who regularly sells out there? We know the workers don't come into town often during harvest, but that's the time when they have the most money. Maybe he does a delivery run." Clarice is running her fingers though her hair, developing an unattractive do.

Something is clicking over in my brain. "Wait...what if *Angel* is the dealer? She uses her trips to both see clients and deliver drugs."

Now Clarice's eyes light up. "What if she's a runner and picks up drugs at the camp to bring back? She's a full-service provider."

We look at each other. Either of these scenarios could work. Angel has been a fixture in town for several years.

Everybody knew about her, but she kept a low profile and didn't flaunt her business, either sex or her habit. Since I've been in Monroe, I'd never seen a soliciting arrest for her.

"How are we going to find out about this? The cops are keeping a tight rein on their investigation, the *jefe* wouldn't talk even if he knew. What about her family?"

"I'm not comfortable asking her dad if he knew she was dealing drugs." Clarice is paling at the prospect. "I have another appointment to talk to him tomorrow about how they scheduled an intervention and how it worked—or I guess didn't work. I'll go as far as asking him if he knew where she got her drugs. That may shake something loose."

I agree with her. Between us, we have great theories, but are woefully short of actual knowledge of how this stuff happens. Except for a couple of dabbles with marijuana in college, I'm a virgin where any hard dugs are concerned and I suspect Clarice is the same. This isn't a topic I've discussed with her and something I don't want to know. Her plan sounds good to me.

On the way out of my office she turns. "You know, I had a funny feeling when I was talking to *jefe*."

I never pooh-pooh her funny feelings. She has some off-the-wall ideas, but all of them are worth at least hearing through. "What kind of feeling?"

"He was bothered...no, that's not the right word..." She reaches up to scratch her head, feels the mess there and tries to finger-comb it back into submission. "He was nervous, almost frightened."

Hmmm. I watch her trail back to her desk

She's finished her first story on Angel, her family and the destruction that her life brought to all the others. It's good. I slot it to run Sunday and send it, along with a budget for the other stories to come in the next week, to the feature's editor at the San Francisco *Times* with a cc to Phil. I send Clarice a "Well done!" note and tell her I've sent it over. then go home to Mac.

CHAPTER TWENTY-NINE

Monday morning I have a blizzard of emails and a stack of "While you were out" notes. It seems Clarice's story on the Bonham family has struck a chord. Several of them, and discordant ones, as well.

There are ones commenting on what a great story it was. Kudos on painting a rounded picture of Angel/Jesse and making her and her family human. Congratulations on how well-written it was.

And the ones that say we are going to burn in hell for taking up space to write such crap about a hooker and a drug addict. Several subscription cancellations because "I thought you were a family newspaper. I won't let MY family read this!"

I suspected this might happen and I'm heartened to see that the accolades are running two-to-one in favor. I know that most of the people who like and approve of the story won't write, but the antis will come out in force. I'm figuring the true balance is closer to five-to-one and chances are the cancellations will be back, if for nothing more than the weekly grocery ads.

Clarice is head-down today, writing the draft of her intervention story. I can hear her on the phone at one point talking to an interventionist from Sacramento. I've forwarded some of the better emails to her and she's on a well-deserved high, even helping Steve write a lede for a short piece on an arraignment he covered.

One of the emails this afternoon is from Phil, who adds his congratulations and says the editor was pleased. "He's holding it to run as a package when you file the other stories, but agreed it should be a contest entry." I forward a copy of this to Clarice as well and watch her head pop up. She looks like a well-content cream-eating cat.

There's still enough light left in the sky to see the note tucked under the wiper blade. I get so tired of people trying to sell stuff, refinance my house or, worse, trying to entice me to the newest gym. I drag it off and crumple it then notice it's really a note.

"Don't mess where you shouldn't."

Unsigned.

Of course.

I've gotten these before but they always shake me. I hotfoot it down to the Monroe Police Department to talk to the detective on duty who assures me that it's probably some crank and makes a comment about running a story that sanitizes a drug-using prostitute. He does take a report though and says he'll have patrols swing by the paper's parking lot randomly.

Once home and with Mac walked, I check all the locks and shut the sliding glass door. Usually I keep it open both for Mac and for fresh air. A breeze comes up through the Delta in the evening and cools the house off before I go to bed.

Clarice has filed a draft of her intervention story. It's good, but not as much of a stand-out as her Bonham one. This is more technical and less personal. She's quoted Samuel Bonham about their session with Jesse/Angel and an interventionist who says that there are always those who fail, adding that some people just aren't ready to give up their addiction, whatever it is.

I'm restless and nervy. To slow my brain down, I pull a pound or so of the information from the Wine Institute and spread it across the kitchen table. This isn't holding as much interest now that the allure of drugs is sprinkled over the Vineyard Murders, but vines and wines are still a big part of Monroe's economy and culture, so any research is a good thing.

It's close to 11 p.m. when the statistics on acres, crop yields, gallons, dollars and market share start do-si-do-ing around my eyes. I let Mac out for the last time and crawl into bed with a new Elizabeth George. Murder in the English countryside is far enough removed from our vineyards that the book hits the floor after a few pages as I fall asleep.

The morning TV news doesn't have anything new but does have a trailer for an "Excusive Interview with a Murder Victim's Family at 6 p.m." I guess the fact that we ran Clarice's story doesn't count in broadcast land. It's exclusive because the other stations didn't think of it first.

When Clarice comes in, she's subdued. I ask her what's up and she comes in my office and closes the door. Oh-oh.

"There was a note on my car when I left last night," she says.

"What kind of note?" I don't know why I'm asking, I know what kind, but a casual conversation may take some of the scare out of it.

"It was just printed on a sheet of copy paper, folded over and stuck under my wiper blade. It said, 'Stay away from the labor camp if you know what's good for you.'"

Oooooh, that's a lot more explicit than mine, which I tell her about before we both make a beeline for the cops.

We talk to the detective from yesterday, Harry Beloit, who begins to look more concerned. He takes Clarice's note for forensic testing, but holds out no hope. It's plain copier paper, six dollars a ream at discount office supply stories, typed in twelve-point Times New Roman, default font of just about every PC, and probably no fingerprints. He does agree with us that the specifics about the labor camp make it more ominous than my "Keep out" but thinks they're tied together and promises to have a patrol guy stationed in our lot for the next few days.

Out of the police office, we look at each other and telegraph "Jim Dodson". Normally we wouldn't ask him to step on the local cops' toes but we've done our duty by reporting it to them and now we need to talk to the guys who're actually handling the murder investigations.

I call Dodson as we're on our way. Wonder of wonders, he's in and doesn't have anyone with him so says "Come on over." Once in his office, we both start at once, then stop, then start again. He grins. "OK, I'll be traffic cop. You start, Amy."

I tell him about my note, which of course I've left with Beloit, then Clarice recites hers. Also with Beloit. I don't think that's a problem as there's no way they'd be traceable. Dodson agrees.

"They're not traceable, but they're definitely tied together and into what's happening with DeFazio. We need to get this to the task force."

"I don't want to talk to that DEA guy again." I just have a feeling he'll put it down to a harmless prank and I don't want to be brushed off. Clarice and I aren't usually scaredy-cats and we wouldn't have brought it up if it seemed harmless.

I'm a little chagrinned when I think back to the first threat I got in the mail. I did overreact, demanded the cops fingerprint the letter and follow up on the return address. It wasn't until they pointed out that the letter-writer included his address that I began to see it was a crank. Now I'm judicious when I cry "Wolf" but these two require a harder look.

"You won't have to talk to Skies again. I'd like you both to come to a task force meeting for a few minutes tomorrow morning and go over the letters and your activities. It's only a precaution. If they're all tied together everybody needs to be on the same page."

Oh Lord, the sheriff's been spending too much time with the feds. He's using the jargon.

CHAPTER THIRTY

To keep the peace, Dodson calls the Monroe detective, Beloit, and tells him that Clarice and I have been invited to talk to the task force. All on the same page, as he said.

Skies puts out his icy stare as we walk into the conference room that's become the group's home. He's turned the white boards to the wall and covered everything else. Somebody's been at work. Four phones and five laptops are scattered across the big table, chairs have been pushed back and paper coffee cups lurch drunkenly out of the trash. There's a faint scent of male perspiration and aftershave, not enough to pin down a brand.

In addition to Dodson, Skies and Beloit, four other men are standing around, looking like we interrupted a discussion...or maybe a joke-telling session. Nope, these guys don't seem as though they'd enjoy jokes.

We're introduced. Dodson prefaces it with "Both Ms. Hobbes and Ms. Stamms have been cooperative when we've needed to go public and ask for help and have agreed to keep our conversations this morning completely off the record."

Skies begins which lets us know that he's the ranking agent. "What made you come forward now?"

Oh good, his reaction to me has changed...not. Should we have come forward *before* we got notes on our cars?

"I have veiled threats a lot of the time because I'm the most visible person in charge at the *Press*. People don't like what the news is, their first thought is to try and kill the messenger. This one was specific enough that I thought I'd report it to the Monroe police."

" 'Keep out' is specific?" Skies isn't buying it.

"It's specific because it was on my car. Most of the threats I get are phone calls or letters to the office along the lines of 'You better start running the truth' or 'Stop covering up for the police'. Those are cranks. I just toss them."

Now Clarice takes over. Her body English says "Don't be an ass" but her voice says "Mine was pretty specific. Whoever wrote it knows I've been out at the labor camp."

"What do yours usually say?" Skies turns his blue icicles on the blond. I think he wants to discredit us as a couple of nervous broads and his disdain drips into the room.

He should know better than to take Clarice on. Her look rivets him to the floor. "I wouldn't know. I've never gotten one before."

A choked sound in the room. I think somebody is trying to stifle a laugh. I don't turn to look. If it's Dodson, I don't want to embarrass him in front of his peers, but I have a small warm spot for the choker.

Skies regroups. "If you've never received a threat, why get one now? What were you doing at the labor camp?"

"I was talking to the field boss. You may have noticed I'm writing a series on Angel, her family, her problems with drugs. I thought he'd know why she was out there, and he did."

"He's one of our witnesses. What did you talk to him about? You better not interfere with an ongoing investigation." Color was starting to climb up Skies neck, but there was no warmth in his eyes.

"If you'd read my story, it was part of the sidebar. He told me she went out every so often to meet with her regulars."

He's not mollified. "What else did you talk about?"

OK, now we're treading way too close to the First Amendment press rights. I need to step in. "Agent Skies, you know that Clarice can't and won't tell you information that she may or may not have that came from a source and isn't already published. Are you asking for her notes?"

Now the flush is up to his ears and it's clearly from anger. He'd love to see her notes. He'd love to get her in an interrogation room. He'd love to have her subpoenaed. But he can't. He knows it's only a fishing expedition and whatever information she has, it's not enough to pull out any big guns. And boy, is he pissed.

I smile at him. "Agent Skies, Clarice and I both know there isn't a chance you'll be able to use these notes we found on our cars, they're just too generic. We wanted to bring them to you in case they could help in any way." I look at Dodson. "Does anyone else want to talk to us?"

The muscles around Dodson mouth are wanting to get active in a big grin. He shakes his head and they quiet down as he says, "I don't think so Amy. Will you and Ms. Stamms be in the office today in case any questions come up?"

Clarice and I exchange a glance. "Unless there's some breaking news."

We nod a goodbye, stick our hands out for a shake from Skies, who doesn't dare snub us, and leave.

Outside, we break into nervous giggles. "What an ass!" Clarice says as she takes a breath. "I'd hate to have him on my tail, he'd hound like Inspector Javet in Les Miz."

"Yep, I agree. He does have a one-track mind. And no sense of humor."

"I'm so glad he asked me what else I talked to *jefe* about. It gave you the perfect opportunity to nail him on First Amendment issues."

"Be careful around him, Clarice. He may be the type who'd try a subpoena just because he doesn't like that we don't have to tell him everything."

There's a blinking light when I come into my office. This is probably not good news. Most people will either leave a message with the newsroom clerk or call my cell if it's urgent. It takes a second to place the voice as that of Samuel Bonham and as I'm listening to the message, I frantically wave Clarice into my office.

"What? You look like a football referee. Why are you waving your arms?"

"It's a message from Bonham. Listen." I punch the button again, and his voice is in the office. "Ms. Hobbes, I don't want to alarm you, but we've had some vandalism. Somebody threw a rock through our front room window last night and my wife is at the vet right now with our dog. We think he's been poisoned. Should we report this to the police?"

CHAPTER THIRTY-ONE

In the space of a few minutes we've gone from being the scourge of law enforcement to the guru of law and order. Clarice says "Do you want to call him or should I?"

"I'll call him. Then when it's a police report, you pick it up and get some comment on it."

When he answers the phone, his voice is quiet. He doesn't sound frightened, just resigned.

"I'm so sorry for all the trouble, Mr. Bonham. Absolutely, you need to report this to the police. It's probably just some of the people who didn't like that we ran Jesse's story. I should have thought and warned you about them. Do you still have the rock?"

"I do. It's still on the living room floor. We haven't touched it. We wondered if there might be fingerprints on it. I was hoping you'd get back to me soon. We'd like to get this mess cleaned up and the window replaced."

I shoot a glance at Clarice. "I think the sooner you get the police out there, the faster you'll be able to get things back to normal. How's your dog?"

"The vet gives him a fifty-fifty chance of making it. We were lucky that he'd only been outside for a few minutes when he ate whatever it was. He started vomiting and frothing and my wife got him in the car while I called the vet's office. The doctor says if he pulls through it'll be because we acted so quickly." Now I hear a catch in his voice. "We've had Grady for seven years. We got him at the shelter when he was a puppy. He's our family now."

"Again, I'm so sorry, Mr. Bonham."

"Thank you but it wasn't anything you've done. We had to get Jesse's story out there if we have any chance of catching her murderer. I'll call the police now."

I sit back and watch Clarice gather up her purse, cell and notebook again. "Give it a few minutes before you check the cops logs, Clar. It'll be awkward if they know we're playing first responder. What a decent, stand-up guy. A lot of people in Bonham's place would be yelling and screaming that we caused the damage. Probably demanding that the *Press* pay for the new window and the vet's bill. My heart aches for him."

She's bouncing her keys in her hand and the jarring noise is giving me a headache as well. I glare at the keys, she picks up the vibe, catches them mid-throw and puts them in her pocket. I smile.

"It's close to time for my usual first rounds," she says. "If I'm late, they'll wonder what's up." She's out the door.

This is curiouser and curiouser as Alice said. There are still three bodies that may or may not be related murders. There are tons of expensive grapes waiting to be harvested. There are drugs floating around that probably shouldn't be where they are. And now there's a perfectly nice family of a victim who are being victimized again for telling her story. Life just isn't fair.

I'm not the type to go whining to a man, but I suddenly have a great need to let Phil know what's happening. I send him an email with a quick outline of the notes on our cars, a biased recap of our conversation with Skies this morning, and a bit about my conversation with Samuel Bonham.

Skies' comments and behavior have made me a touch antsy

about discoverability on email and phone calls. I don't want anything that could come back to bite me, the *Press* or Phil should anything happen and search warrants are executed. It would all be beyond the scope, except for the notes, and those put Clarice and me out of the objective roles of media and into the subjective roles of victims.

I end the email by couching it as a discussion and questions about what the *Times* will want in Clarice's stories. The threats to us are no-nos but the vandalism at the Bonham's may be part of a larger story.

The "you have a message" sounds as I'm reading the local copy for tonight and I open an email back from Phil. He says the *Times* is interested in the overall stories and if the vandalism becomes part of that, sure they're interested. If it's just part of the backlash from having Jesse's story made public, then no; "that's just the price of fame, LOL."

He also tells me to take care of myself, an oddly worded sign-off that makes me think he was reading between the lines after he read my version of Skies. Even though there was very little personal in the exchange, I feel better, more centered, now that someone, someone outside of Monroe, someone who's not involved in any of this, knows what's happened.

Clarice is back from the cops with the notes about the Bonham's vandalism and is off to talk to him.

Apparently he did turn the rock over and the cops are taking it seriously enough that they're running it for prints. It will be a day or so before anything shows up. And even if they do get prints, then what?

Fingerprints alone won't tie the rock-through-the-window to either someone warning them off about looking for Jesse's murderer or just someone pissed about their daughter's life choices. When Clarice comes back we have a short tussle over whether this is a big story, a story or just a brief.

I finally pull rank and it becomes a brief.

"Look, Clarice, what would you do with this if it was random vandalism against someone we don't know? You'd never write it as more than a brief...and on a hot news day, not even that. We've already stuck our heads up and had a warning shot, let's not make ourselves targets over something we can't tie to squat."

"Are you afraid?"

"No, but we open ourselves up to grandstanding if we let our involvement become part of the story. The reason we're concerned about Bonham's window is because we assume it might be tied to our warnings."

I'm not sure she sees this reasoning, but the incident remains a brief and her notes get tucked away, pending any resolutions that might be beyond a simple prank.

It's been a long day. My mind is scattered. When I get home, I change, thinking a walk with Mac will be calming. We head out the door, into our usual walk, walk faster, stop, back up, run ahead pattern. My stress is coming down a notch with the routine until my cell rings and Phil is asking me what really happened.

My voice is maybe a little shaky because he says, "Do you want me to come over?"

Oh god, I don't want to play the distressed damsel. "No, no, I'm just tired and that routine with the DEA guy, Skies, was a bunch of wasted energy. I know I shouldn't let him get to me. I sure didn't want him seeing that I was concerned about the car notes, I don't ever want to play victim with him."

"Won't your pal the sheriff watch your back?"

"He will and he does, but Skies—and the FBI guys, who seem strangely quiet—outrank him. He has to play his own politics as well."

"Huh, it all comes down to that pecking order, doesn't it. What's happening with the vine/wine research? Any conclusions?"

"No conclusions. It's still useful, but I'm beginning to think this drug stuff..."

We've reached the Schnauzers' house and Mac is trying to

wrap himself around me to hide when suddenly I'm in the air, then stumbling, trying to get my balance, then nothing.

CHAPTER THIRTY-TWO

Something's not right. I hurt. All over. My head, my arm, my back. The skin on my legs is on fire.

There's a guy shouting at me. "Are you all right? Can you hear me? Can you talk?"

I have no idea. Then, "I don't know. Where am I?"

"You're on the sidewalk in front of my house. It was terrible. I've called 911."

I start to lift my head up and decide that it's not a good idea. At all. Something wet and warm is tricking down behind my ear. Am I bleeding? Bleeding from your ear is never a good sign. Then I realize the wet is accompanied by a soft snuffle. Mac is licking me. And one of the Schnauzers lets out a yelp. I know where I am. And the voice must be the Schnauzers' owner.

Things start to come back. I was taking Mac for a walk and talking to Phil on my cell.

Phil! Where's my phone?

"Where's my phone" I yell at the Schnauzer guy.

"I don't know. It must have flown out of your hand when the car hit you."

A car hit me?

"How did a car hit me? And where is it?"

"I didn't see where it came from, I just heard the thud, looked up and saw you bouncing over the hood. Then it took off again. Please just lay still until the ambulance gets here."

I'm beginning to shake. The Schnauzer guy runs into his house. Is he leaving me here to bleed out or whatever on his sidewalk? No, he comes running back out with a chenille throw off his couch.

"Here, you're shivering."

Somebody must have been sitting on the throw because it's nice and warm and I'm drifting when I hear the sirens.

Dear god, it's everybody. Fire, police followed by the ambulance. The fire guys are first, checking my breathing, shining a flashlight in my eyes, running their hands up and down my legs and arms.

"Can you hear us? Can you talk?" What I want to say is that I just went through this patter, but I nod my head. Big mistake. When I let out the moan, they really begin to move. By then the ambulance is there and all the paramedics get me on a backboard, put a cervical collar on me, get an IV line and a blood pressure cuff started as the two cops are asking questions.

"Do you know what happened?"

"This man told me I was hit by a car." I have to roll my eyes at the Schnauzer guy because I can't move my head or arms with all the equipment I'm wearing.

"What were you doing? Did you hear the car?"

"No, I didn't hear anything. I was walking my dog and talking to a friend...wait, wait, where's my phone? My friend must have heard it. He'll be worried."

"Is this it?" The Schnauzer guy hands my battered phone to one of the cops who punches a few buttons. "Still working, good thing it landed on the lawn. Do you have any identification? What's your name?"

"My name is Amy Hobbes. I don't have any identification with me."

"Where do you live? Is there anyone at home we can talk to?"

"No, I live alone."

Suddenly the cop who's not asking questions bolts for the cruiser and grabs his cell phone. I can't hear his conversation because the paramedics are getting me and all my gear onto a gurney. The cop comes back, he and his partner have a fast whispered conversation and the questioner says "We'll continue this at the hospital."

Hospital? I don't want to go to the hospital. I just want my phone and to finish my conversation with Phil. And what about Mac? Somewhere along the line I let go of his leash, but he's not leaving me. In fact, he tries to jump into the ambulance with me, not easy with his short legs and the Schnauzer guy now tugging on his leash.

"No, Mac. You have to stay. These nice men will take you home." Good thing he understands my tone.

In fact, the Schnauzer guy says, "He can stay here for a while. These fools," he waves at the Schnauzers, now mercifully silent, "are just big babies. They'll shut up." He turns to the cops and gives them his name, address and phone number, both as a witness and as a dog custodian.

The paramedics lock my gurney in, get themselves settled, hang the bag that's dripping into my arm and off we go. I don't rate lights-and-siren as I'm awake and talking with no visible bleeding—and we're only eight blocks from the hospital. Once at the ER, I discover the benefits to coming in by ambulance. The emergency room has taken the place of a family doctor for some people but ambulance arrival zooms to the top of the triage list. By the time I'm settled in a cubicle, it looks like a party. The paramedics are giving a report to the nurse, the fire guys have come along as well and there are now four cops—two patrol and two detectives—wanting to get my story.

I tell them what I remember, which isn't much. Monroe has chosen to use rolled curbs in the residential neighborhoods rather than the straight ones. They help with water runoff, give a bit more room for parking and are easier to maneuver for wheeled things like strollers, wheelchairs, bicycles—and cars. It turns out that whoever hit me had come up on the sidewalk through a curb cut and just rolled off and away.

And the detectives are there because once the cops found out who I am, they put things together with the car note and upped the ante.

"Are you sure you didn't see or hear anything?" This is the detective I saw at the task force meeting...was that just this morning? He didn't say anything then, but was plenty talkative now. "Mr. Juarez," He stops at my blank look. "The witness? The man who's taking care of your dog?"

Ah, the Schnauzer guy has a name!

"Mr. Juarez was trimming his lawn when he heard a thud, turned to look and saw you falling off the hood of a car. He said it was a black SUV with tinted windows but couldn't see who was driving or get a license plate number. It just hit you and kept on moving. He said it didn't even slow down. It's a residential neighborhood and the driver was only going about twenty-five Juarez estimated. Since they didn't slow down there aren't any skid marks and because all the newer cars have recessed front turn lights, there isn't any glass or plastic. It just vanished, poof..." and he flicked his fingers.

This is cold comfort. I know what the odds are of tracing a hit-and-run with no license plate and no damage. There's not anything else I can tell them.

Just as well, because the doctor finally shows up and I have to tell her the story all over again. She checks my vitals, shines a light in my eyes, feels up and down my arms and legs, tsk-tks over my road-rashed legs and sends me off for a CT scan. When I get rolled back to my cubicle, Clarice is there, trying her damnedest to pace in a six by nine room.

"Whewww, am I glad to see you! You should know better than to talk on your cell and walk at the same time!"

As an attempt at levity, it's about a two, but I do smile. "How'd you get here? Who called you?"

"When the cops figured out who you are, the duty sergeant called me to get your next of kin. I told them Heather but I didn't know her phone number and said I'd come to the hospital and give them all your information. I have your key, so I swung by and picked up your purse." Her rapid delivery slows down and I know she's more concerned than she's letting on. "I hope I did OK."

CHAPTER THIRTY-THREE

"You did just great, Clar. Thank you" She's probably done better than either Heather or Phil would have. There's an attachment between us, but we've bonded as grown-up career friends so don't have as much emotional baggage. "Have you called anyone?"

"No. I brought your address book in case you want to."

"I don't know where my cell phone is. I dropped it when I got hit. One of the cops picked it up and said it was still working, but I don't know what happened to it after that."

"Let me check the bag they brought."

The first responders gather up everything they find that might belong to the person being transported and put in a bag that stays with the gurney. In my case, the bag is almost empty when Clar reaches under the gurney and pulls it out. The only item is my cell phone, bless that cop.

She punches it on, the face lights up and she hands it to me. I have two missed calls, both of them from Phil. As I hit dial, the doctor comes back, so I disconnect and wait for the bad news. Surprisingly little.

"You do have a concussion," she says. "And two cracked ribs. Nothing broken, bad sprain of your left wrist and probably some pulled ligaments in your left leg. Was that the side you landed on?"

I have to think for a minute. "Yes, the car must have come across the lane and hit me from behind. I just remember being in the air, then lying on my side while someone was shouting at me."

She looks at the monitors above my head, makes a note. "We're going to keep you overnight and I'll have an orthopedic guy check your wrist but there's no permanent damage."

Short and sweet. I pick up my phone and hit dial just as it rings. It's Phil. And he's worried...or maybe concerned.

"What happened? I heard 'drugs' then all kinds of crashing noises then voices in the background and then a hang up. Were you grabbed?"

I give him the brief version and that I'm in the hospital overnight.

"Should I come over?" Should he come over and see me scraped and bruised? No, definitely not.

"No, I'm fine, a bit battered. I wanted to tell you why I didn't call you back. Clarice will drive me home tomorrow. She's picking up Mac, taking him home to spend the night."

"If you're sure..."

"I'm sure. It's lovely of you to offer. I really am fine. The next time I see you I want to be whole and well."

Clarice heads out, the transport team shows up, I'm put into a room, the orthopedic guy comes the next morning and gives me a wrap and sling for my wrist, tells me to take it easy, ice my wrist and leg, don't do any strenuous lifting and sends me home.

My body complains getting in and out of the car. I do the stairs, take a shower, look in the mirror and head for bed. I have bruises up and down my legs, not to mention missing skin, there's a big bruise on my left cheek and my eyes are purpling from the concussion. Working from home for a few days.

I call Heather just to let her know and the screeches echo through my sore head. "You were hit by a car? Are you sure you're all right?"

"Yes, I'm fine. My wrist is in a sling and I can't lean over very well. I'm going to work from home for a few days. If you call, leave a message."

In addition to the sling, which will probably cost my insurance company seventeen hundred dollars, I'm sent home with some pain meds. I take one. The next time I open my eyes it's getting dark and there's a figure at my bedroom door. I scream, Mac barks and Clarice flips on the light.

"Remind me why I'm not a home care nurse?"

"Sorry Clar. What's going on?"

"I came by to see how you are and take Mac for a walk if he hasn't been. I'm guessing you've been out of it all day."

I nod, happy to feel only twinges of pain from my head. "Is everything all right at work?"

She gives me a quick rundown, which for Clarice means what's happening at the cops, and tells me they aren't releasing any information about my "accident". Just as well, I don't need to publically become a victim.

"Are you coming in tomorrow?"

"I don't think so. I feel better, but I'd still scare little children." It'll take a few days for the bruising to fade but the swelling should be gone. "Thanks for taking Mac out. I'm planning to walk him tomorrow, I need to get up and move."

Clarice is gone, Mac is sitting by my bed and I'm starving. I roll over, gingerly edge out of bed and head downstairs to find some food. While I'm down, I log on to my email, see some condolences from the staff, the publishers, a few regular readers and sources and a note from Jim Dodson. "I think we need to talk. Call my cell when you feel well enough."

Cryptic. And even ominous.

When I call the next morning he's quiet and sounds concerned. "Are you feeling better?"

I assure him that I'm well, just sore, but I don't ask him the ultimate "why did you call?" He'll tell me.

"You were right to call the Monroe police. I'd like to come over and talk to you about the accident, though. Are you free later today?"

Hmmm, this isn't the usual tone he takes with me, It's as though he's treating me as a witness, or a victim. What's going on? "I'm available all day, I'm working from home."

"Good. I'll see you this afternoon." He's gone. Odd. Not "good-bye", not "thanks", not "see you later".

Mac goes into a barking frenzy when Dodson rings the bell. It takes me longer to get places so he's standing on the mat for a couple of minutes before I get the door open. Although I can't see his eyes behind the dark glasses, I can see his eyebrows arc. He comes in, takes his glasses off and now I can see the concern in his eyes. He closes the door before he speaks.

"You do look battered. I'm so sorry."

It's kind of him to say so. "It's better, even though it may look worse. I hate when bruises get to that yellow stage. It clashes with everything."

His lips curl up at my flipness. "I see that it's only on the surface. I wanted to talk to you without anyone else. And not on a land line or through email."

Now I'm concerned. What is he telling me, that he thinks there's some conspiracy involved? Or that he's working with someone he doesn't trust. Or, most likely, he has information that he hasn't released to any one?

CHAPTER THIRTY-FOUR

We move to the kitchen overlooking the pool and I offer an iced tea. He looks like he'd rather have a Coke, but I don't keep carbonated drinks around and he takes the tea with thanks.

"This is very nice Amy." he says, casting around at the family room that opens out to the backyard and pool through French doors. "Have you lived here long?"

The subtext; "Boy, they must pay you a lot at the *Press*!"

He takes a stool at the kitchen's island, drops his sunglasses and punches his phone to vibrate. "You can see as well as anyone that these incidents are related."

Incidents? Cop-speak is crazy-making. "Which incidents? Is murder an incident?"

With a grimace, he nods. "Yes, bodies are incidents, traffic accidents are incidents, vandalism and hit-and-run are incidents. You're looking like an incident waiting to happen."

"Thanks for the analysis. What can I do about it?"

There's a small silence, then "Remember when I took you to the gun range?"

"Of course I remember, I asked you to."

"Have you thought more about buying a gun?"

"Not a lot, no. Why?"

Now he stares out at the pool, looking like he's trying to make up his mind or find the right words. "I don't recommend people running out to arm themselves. Too many gun shot wounds and killings happen as it is. You were married to a cop, you know the damage. Right now you're the target. Why? By whom?" He shrugs. "We're working to find out. The feds are pinning a lot of supposition on drugs. Me, I'm not fully convinced."

Is he giving me hints about the way the investigation is headed?

"This isn't based on any new facts. It's my emotional, gut reaction. There's no rationale behind it, so don't start looking for new leads."

OK, not a different path...but he's able to figure out the way my mind is working. I pick up a sponge and swipe at invisible spots on the island while my brain churns through the reasons he's talking about a gun.

"Well, if it's not drugs, what is it?"

"Oh, sure, Amy. I'll tell you how things went down, we'll take it to the DA for charging and you'll have a nice page one package for Clarice. I don't think so."

Guess I hit too close to the bone. Backpedaling, "No. I'm sure if you knew how the pieces fit together you'd be at the DA's office, not here. I'm curious about the drugs, too. It doesn't seem like an international ring would be here, in Monroe. I've always thought this was a local event."

"I'm leaning toward the local event angle as well. A professional hit, the car would be going fast enough to make sure you were dead. And probably wouldn't have headed for you in a residential neighborhood with witnesses. It smacks of amateurs wanting it to really look like an accident. And they upped the ante from a note on your windshield."

Something has been wiggling around in the back of my brain and now it wings its way into consciousness. I remember what I was doing when the tox screen information dragged my attention to drugs.

"I didn't tell you about my Davis research." I fill him in on what I've found about the grapes grown here—especially the values.

His eyebrows rise as I do the math and he realizes it can be millions of dollars annually. "That's a home-grown motive for murder."

Then I decide to open up and tell him about my conversation with Nesman at the Chamber. I'm honest enough to preface it with my reactions to the man and even use the word "smarmy".

Dodson laughs. "I think he's a bit unctuous. I've put it down to him reacting to law enforcement and me being higher than him in the pecking order. He probably feels he can get away with condescension with you, you're only a woman."

I'm stunned, then I see Dodson's eyes crinkle with laughter. "Only a woman? Yep, but I work for a company that buys ink by the barrel!" I tell him that I sensed another phone hanging up at the end of Nesman's conversation.

"Did you hear something, or was it a feeling?"

"I heard something like a click. I wouldn't have thought too much about it except for Nesman gasping when I mentioned doing research at Davis."

Dodson swirls melting ice and a battered lemon slice around in his glass. "That's a little odd, even for him. Let me know about any other conversations."

It's been comforting to talk to Dodson in a relaxed setting, but there's still that question hanging around like the proverbial elephant. Have I thought any more about buying a gun? I have. I'm not usually nervous and I went as far as I usually do the other night when I locked the house up.

Today, just a glance in the mirror reminds me that someone is after me. It's not an easy feeling.

He looks directly at me. "Well, have you thought about it?"

Is he exhibiting some weird sort of ESP? Am I giving off

an aura of neediness? Head-slap, Amy. He'd asked me a question, we'd danced around it with conversation and now he's asking again.

"I have thought about it. Until a few days ago, I'd have said 'No. That's not a step I want to take.' Now..." I shake my head, gently. The residual fuzziness and ache change my mind.

"Now, I think, yes. I've been warned and I can't ignore these threats. It wouldn't have helped the other night and I'm not planning to carry one around with me, but I'll feel safer if I know I have one in the house."

Dodson shifts on his stool. "I was hoping you'd change your mind. There are too many 'incidences'", he smiles as he puts air quotes around the word.

I pick up our glasses and move them to the sink. A gun. I'm going to buy a gun. I can feel that Vinnie's pleased with my decision, probably more so than I am.

"Would you help me with it?" I look at Dodson. If I have a gun in the house, I want to be sure I know how to use it and use it the right way.

He nods. "Of course. We'll find the time to get back to the gun range and set up a series of lessons. When are you going back to work?"

"Tomorrow. Could you schedule a late lunch?"

Dodson picks up his sunglasses and digs his keys out. "I can manage that if nothing blows up. I'll call you."

I see him to the door, close it and lean against it. "Mac, you've been the best protection I've ever had and you're still going to be number one. But it looks like we're going to be armed...and not dangerous."

This time when I lean over to give him a head-scrub, my head feels fine.

CHAPTER THIRTY-FIVE

Hmmm. I may have over-estimated my healing a tad.

Even with the ear protectors, the noise in the gun range makes my head throb with each shot.

Jack has two Glocks ready when Dodson and I show up. He smiles at me. "Does this mean you've made up your mind?"

"I think so. Sheriff Dodson and I have been talking and it's a good step."

He makes me go over the loading of the magazines, inserting and ejecting them, safety on, safety off, safety on, safety off, shooting. "Don't snap the trigger, squeeze it. You'll get better aim and the gun won't jerk so much which means you'll have a better chance of hitting what you're aiming at."

His advice sounds like patronizing hoo-hah, until I try it his way and, surprise, surprise, I hit the target.

Dodson's watching and suppresses a smile. "You didn't wing them, Amy, but you probably scared the hell out of them."

"I'm glad you two are having fun! I'm going to have to practice at this."

"Everybody does, at first." Jack loads another magazine.

"How often do you want to come?"

With the way my head feels, the answer is "Never".

We leave it with twice-weekly appointments and until my permit clears, Jack will loan me a Glock to use.

Outside, Dodson and I shake hands. "I imagine this wasn't an easy step Amy, but I'm glad you took it. We still have no leads on the car or driver who hit you. Dark SUVs with tinted windows..." He doesn't have to finish that sentence.

Back at work, there's a steady stream of *Press* employees by my office. Wishing me well but I suspect wanting to see how bad I look. Better, but I was right. The yellow is unattractive and make-up doesn't cover it, a wrist brace instead of the sling and no sudden torso turns.

Today, there's Clarice's story on drug trafficking in the Central Valley with a sidebar on meth production. She had a good interview with Skies who's unbent a little when treated as an expert. I tag them to run and send a copy to Phil and to the features editor at the *Times*.

Phil's back immediately. "Are you at work Amy? How are you feeling?"

I tell him fine and lose an argument with myself over telling him about my gun purchase. I sense guns aren't in Phil's reference scheme. There'll be plenty of time to tell him when he comes over to spend the night again.

I'm on the phone with Samuel Bonham when Clarice storms in. Grady, the Bonham's dog, pulled through and is now an indoor pet, only going out on a leash. "He thinks he's being punished, but we don't dare lose sight of him until all this goes away," Bonham says as I watch steam coming out of Clarice's ears.

"I'm so glad he's well, Mr. Bonham. Please let us know if the police track down any suspects." I wave Clarice in and shut the door.

"What?"

She's completely skipped several shades and is now at cherry. "That asshole, that scum, that rotten SOB..."

"Tell me what you really think and who you're talking about."

"Skies." She spits his name out. "That two-faced rat..."

"Whoa...! I read your story. It sounded as though he'd given you some good information. What happened?"

She slams herself into a chair so hard it groans in pain. "I was over at the Sheriff's department and just stuck my head in the task force room to say hello and he said 'Where's the story?' I said, 'What story?' and he said 'The one about drug trafficking'."

The he said/she saids are harder to follow than a tennis match. "Slow down, give me the gist."

"That..." It must be bad if Clarice can't come up with a foul name. She starts again, "That...fool, says 'I have to read it first.'. I was so angry I didn't know what to say so I just left! How could he not know about prior restraint?"

Well, that's a good question. We always assume that someone at that level in government knows they can't read the story before it appears, just like they know they can't see any notes or information that doesn't appear in the story.

"Why did he think he could read your story?"

She beetles her eyebrows. "He gave me some cock-and-bull line about national security being at stake and terrorist activities."

National security? Terrorists activities? Here in Monroe?

"Calm down, take a breath, and yes, I'm doing much better."

At that, she sits up and looks at me. "Oh, crap, Amy, I'm sorry. How are you? Besides an interesting shade of yellow?"

Clarice can multi-task occasionally, but when she has a full head of steam it's not the occasion.

I start to lean over my desk and my ribs let me know it's not a good idea. She sees me wince and her chin drops, but I say "I'm OK. I just can't make sudden moves. How do you want us to handle Skies? Besides sic an SUV with tinted windows on him?"

This tiny joke works, she relaxes, the red fades and she leans back. "First, we have to find the right SUV!"

"Do you want me to talk to him?" This isn't a prospect I'm looking forward to. My relations with Mr. Skies aren't much better than hers, but they pay me the big bucks to back up my staff, the *Press* and the First Amendment.

She sighs. Clarice is not someone who expects others to take on her fights. She knows this needs to get kicked up another level though. "I guess you're going to have to, Amy."

Maybe we can pull the sheriff and the Monroe cops in on this as well. It may take some of the sting and venom out of Skies if he can view it as a lesson rather than a reprimand.

"Let's go talk to the Sheriff, I have an idea."

At this, Clarice perks up and even finger-combs her hair.

We're starting to wear a groove in the sidewalk between the *Press* and the Sheriff's office with this case, and the receptionist says "I'll see if he's available."

He is. We're ushered in and he looks at us with a "now what" semi-frown.

I let Clarice tell her story, without pejoratives, and when she's finished, I say, "This is a big problem for us, Sheriff Dodson."

His frown is now full-blown. "I can see that. I'm surprised Skies even thought of trying to read the story first. Apparently the DEA doesn't have a 'How to deal with the press' class."

"Funny you should bring that up, Sheriff. I'm going to suggest that we do one now with all the task force members. We can frame it that this case is growing and getting more attention and we only want to help everyone get out the message they need to."

Dodson smiles at the use of "frame". "When do you want to schedule it?"

I'm thinking yesterday would be nice. "As soon as possible. And I think you should invite a TV station or two as well." Clarice is close enough to me that I feel currents of disgust coming off her. I continue talking to Dodson. "With the TV guys here, Skies and the others won't think that it's just us, the lowly Monroe *Press*, who are having difficulty. It'll help spread the enmity and give Skies more targets for his disdain."

The Sheriff agrees, it's set for tomorrow afternoon, Clarice stops fuming and glaring and we head back down the groove.

CHAPTER THIRTY-SIX

Just to be on the safe side, I put a call in to an attorney in Sacramento. We pay him a monthly retainer to vet stories for us, go over libel law with the staff occasionally and help us out on the few First Amendment issues that crop up.

After 9/11 and the establishment of the Department of Homeland Security, his First Amendment business is growing. People at the federal level are trying to push the envelop of privacy and source protection using the umbrella of national security and terrorism, so I'm glad he's free and will come down.

My first day back at work tires me out. I finish reading all the local copy, have a last meeting with the news editor to finalize story play and head home. I'm still skittery and want to walk Mac before it's full dark. With my luck, the next SUV with tinted windows that comes at me will have its headlights off, too.

The walk is uneventful, except Mr. Juarez is out watering and the Schnauzers start to bark. This time, Mac stands his ground and both Mr. Juarez and I laugh as the Schnauzers back off.

"How are you feeling? You're looking better than the last

time I saw you."

He's a very nice man and a good neighbor and I'm grateful for all the help he gave me. "I'm much better. Today was my first day at work. I'm tired, but feeling stronger. Thanks again for all you did."

"I was glad to help. I'll never forget turning around and seeing you bouncing off that car. Have they found it yet?"

I shake my head then shrug. "No, and I'm not sure they ever will. There are thousands of dark SUVs and all of them have their windows tinted."

Once home, Mac curls up in his dog bed while I watch a couple of mindless TV shows and we call it an early night. While I was feeling sketchy, he was relegated to my bedroom floor but now he takes his rightful place on the bed with me.

Sometimes normal is good.

This morning, I take more time with my hair and makeup and pull on a navy silk blazer and not-quite-khaki linen skirt. I even slip on a pair of navy silk heels, not stilettos but not my usual flats, either. I want to send Mr. Skies and his pals a message that I'm a woman—a woman in charge.

Bruce Kindice, our attorney, shows up at my office right after lunch, ready to explain the First Amendment to the over-eager DEA guys. When we walk into the task force room one TV reporter is already there. Clarice is under orders to play nice and she goes over and says hello. I think she totally got my explanation yesterday that this was a skirmish better attempted with more ammunition than anger.

It takes a few minutes for everyone to drift in after lunch and we get started with introductions. Bless Bruce's heart, he's played this game bunches of times. Skies has stationed himself at what could be the head of the table, but Bruce doesn't sit. He stands by a white board, casually tossing a red marker in his hand. Then he begins.

"As I understand it, Agent Skies, the DEA and the FBI are here in Monroe investigating a possible drug link to three murders. Is that correct?"

Skies gives him a modified stink-eye but admits that that's correct. He begins to add something but Bruce smooths on with, "What is the possible link?"

Skies and the FBI Special Agent exchange glances. Skies wins and says, "The best link of all. Mexican nationals cross the border to work in agriculture. Some come back year after year, so they have friends, family, jobs on both sides. We think some supplement their income as a one-time mule for the Mexican drug cartels. They don't have to do it over and over, one twenty-kilo package a year gives them enough extra to be worth it. And the drug guys like using them because they know the routes. They dump their loads for the waiting Southern California brokers, get paid and hop the bus north to the fields."

Bruce draws an arrow on the whiteboard. "And the DEA and FBI think that one load a year from these guys is enough to warrant a task force?"

The icy-blues stare at Bruce as though they're emitting a death ray. "No, just one load a year isn't enough. We're after the way the network is put together. And we're after whoever the Mexican *jefe* is and who the Southern California *jefe* is."

Now the red arrow is double-ended with a question mark at each end. "So, you have task forces..."

"Wait a minute. There are people from the press here and I won't talk about our plans around them." Skies' team and the FBI guys send out waves of approval.

"Fair enough." Bruce sets the marker down and turns to us. "This is background information only, not on the record. Everybody agree to those ground rules?"

Clarice, the TV reporter and I are all voicing our agreement. We're not here to pull classified information out, we're here to explain our roles.

Bruce picks up with "Now, we understand that there are some drugs possibly coming across the border with the migrant ag workers. That doesn't surprise us. It also doesn't seem that the FBI would be involved. As I understand from the Monroe Press reporter, Agent Skies asked to see her story on the basis of national security and terrorist activity being involved. One load of marijuana or even cocaine is troubling, but isn't jeopardizing national security."

"We're pursuing other angles." The FBI Agent-in-Charge is heard from. "We're certain that the two men found murdered in the grease pit are links in this area's drug distribution network."

"That's probably true. Still, what possible angles are there that make you think any of the stories developed from your presence here has any bearing on national security?"

Skies starts with "It's classified..." but Bruce stops him.

"We don't want details, we don't want classified information. Just a simple statement of why you think some Mexican nationals who may or may not be bringing weed across the border is a security problem."

The FBI agent is swallowing his tongue, trying to get a word out. "It's not that they're smuggling, it's what's happening to the marijuana once it's across the border."

Bruce's, Clarice's and my eyebrows reach for the ceiling. "And what is that?"

"We've traced the SoCal contact to the major gangs—the Mexican Mafia, the Crips, the Bloods. They deal in all drugs, not only the ones coming across this border. They deal with suppliers around the world. The poppy fields throughout Asia and the Middle East fund the Taliban and other terrorist groups. There's our target."

It seems a pretty tenuous thread to tie all this together. I know we're not getting the full story. I suspect even the various federal agencies don't share their information and informants. And it sure doesn't seem enough of a link to supersede the rulings on prior restraint and First Amendment rights.

Bruce picks up the red marker again and rolls it between his palms. Why do I feel like it's Skies' neck? His voice is reasonable. "I understand how this is interwoven, Agent Skies, but I need to help you understand a few of the issues that the press has with information."

I hear a muffled sound. One of the other DEA officers is whispering and I catch, "Yeah, right!" before Skies zaps them with his icicle stare. They subside like kids caught passing notes.

"I understand the First Amendment, Mr. Kindice. There is also precedence for information that may jeopardize national security."

As far as Skies is concerned, this is the sand line.

Bruce carefully puts the marker down and nods to us. "I think we've reached a point of agreeing to disagree, Mr. Skies. You may want to check with your Justice Department attorneys, but as of now, I'm advising my clients that the rulings on prior restraint and privacy of sources and their information trump any possible threat of national security."

The TV reporter hasn't said a word until now, when she says "Thank you" to Bruce.

We troop out.

CHAPTER THIRTY-SEVEN

Clarice is squirming like a five-year-old with a secret.
I drill into her wide-open eyes with a simple message, "Not now," and she calms. She even manages to shake the TV woman's hand and remembers to say thank you to Bruce.
Everybody heads off. "Want to go get a coffee?" I ask. She'll crack her neck nodding yes.
We pick a place off the main street, deserted this time of day, and grab a table outside. Drinks in hand I say, "Yes, Clarice. We have a lot of leads to follow up on."
She's running her hands through her hair, lining up the thoughts but finally the dam bursts. "That idiot thinks we have drug kingpins right here in Monroe who are sending money to the Taliban? What's he been smoking?" The raspberry sound she gives spits coffee out and drops land on her shirt.
"You're jumping as fast as he is, Clar. Slow down. He didn't say anyone here is sending money to terrorists, he said that some of the money made off the drugs finds its way there. And I can see that. Those federal guys are looking for all the links that could lead them back to the big dealers. They've been trying to get the gang conduits shut down for

years. If drugs are involved here, it might be another link."

"Why are you defending those jerks?"

The blond's world is black and white—either you're with her or against her and subtlety can be lost on her. "I'm not defending them. I think they have a fruitless job and I guess I'm not always upset when they get rabid about things. I don't like Skies and he's way out of line on this prior restraint but I sure wouldn't want his job."

"And look at all the information he's given us!" I say, with just a trace of sarcasm.

"Like what?" She's getting truculent.

"OK, we know there's a supply line to Southern California and that line has the usual weed and coke and also heroin. This may be where Angel got hers. And she could have easily been the conduit for bringing the drugs back into Monroe."

Clarice's eyes are lighting up. She's tried to scrub the coffee spots out of her shirt and only made larger, paler places that she's dabbing at. "If her customers at the camp were some of the field workers, plus an occasional blow job with *jefe*, she could have stumbled on some information, or even a batch of drugs."

"Exactly. She needed to get put out of the way. Or, she was getting paid with some of the heroin that was coming through the camp and blabbed about where she got her drugs."

"I don't see her as the blabbing type." Clarice is scratching her head with a coffee stirrer. I hope it's an unused one. "She had a lot of different clients and I don't think she ever mixed them up or told who they were."

The smells of roasting coffee and hot milk are reminding me that lunch was a carton of yogurt, downed before the task force meeting. "I'm going to grab a salad and take it back. Bruce made it clear that your story is ready to run, so why don't you visit the camp again?"

Now she's getting as pale as the coffee spots. "Amy, is that a good idea? My note said stay away from the camp."

"Maybe you can meet with the workers in *jeje's* office? They could have reasons for talking to him during harvest."

"I'll give him a call." I realize she *is* nervous, this isn't her usual go-get-'em attitude.

I send an edited version of our meeting with the task force to both Phil and the features editor at the San Francisco *Times*, letting them know they may get some blowback from it, and in a second there's a "Ha, ha, ha!" note back. Journalists are concerned with the new parameters being carved out by Homeland Security and the AG's office and there's talk of possibly phones tapped and emails read. I can remember some older newspaper people telling stories of the Nixon years and how no one ever listened to Martha Mitchell when she'd call the Atlanta *Constitution*.

With the feds admission that they were looking at all the drug links, we do need to ask more questions and talk to more people. I'm certainly not going to put any of the *Press'* limited resources onto a story of how drugs in Monroe might be funding the Taliban. I can, though, call some friends still working in the L.A. area and dig around in their knowledge.

By the time I pack it up to head home, I've talked to two cops reporters—one in the San Fernando Valley and one at the LA *Times*—who tell me that gang violence is down slightly. Neither is sure why and their sources at the various police departments aren't sure either. The *Times* reporter hazards a guess that things on the street are more organized now; territories clearly defined, suppliers lined up for a steady flow and independents run out of the business.

He's quick to add that he doesn't think there are any fewer drugs being sold, just that the supply chain is solidified.

When I ask them if they've ever heard about ties to the Taliban or to terrorist groups they say it's a constant rumor.

Taxon, with the Times, says "Who knows, it could be true. Probably in the overall scheme, profits from the poppies in Afghanistan go to the Taliban. Does that translate to them having a pipeline into the LA drug gangs...? It's possible, but we're so far down the food chain that we'd never get it confirmed."

I whip my notes—questions, answers, suppositions, more questions—into a note and email it to Clarice. She'll see it when she checks back in to do the last cop calls.

A thought hits me that I'm dumping a lot on her. I think I may have underestimated how much the case is affecting her. Taken all together she's had the killings, the truck accident, the murders in the grease pit the emotional scenes with Samuel Bonham, the threatening note on her car and has rolled with it all like a trouper.

I call her cell which goes directly to voice mail. She's probably turned it off during her interviews in *jefe's* office. I leave her a message that I'm assigning Steve to do the late cop calls and for her to head home when she finishes up at the camp.

Then I call Steve in and let him know his new assignment. He's happy...not only does he get to do the cop calls, something he's enjoying, but he'll get a couple of hours of overtime as well.

His overtime won't blast a hole in the newsroom finances. If I have to, I'll take on the *Press'* publishers, Calvin and Max, as well. We're covering a big story, Clarice is writing award-worthy stories, the San Francisco *Times* is picking them up and I'm still keeping the bottom line. I won't even go into why we're in the news business with them, their priority is finances.

Tonight I have to stop for groceries. With the "incident" I haven't felt like I want to tackle routine chores, but now I'm out of staples including coffee and Mac is eating dry food, not his favorite as I usually mix it with canned.

I'm hauling the last bag in from the car when my cell rings. It's Clarice. She's out of breath and her voice is shaky.

CHAPTER THIRTY-EIGHT

"What's going on Clar? Where are you?"
There's background noise and I'm having a hard time hearing her, she's practically whispering.
"I'm just leaving the labor camp and I think somebody's following me! There's a dark SUV behind me. When I pulled out on the highway, it must have been parked on the shoulder because I didn't see anyone coming in my lane."
"Is there any other traffic?"
"There's some."
"Headed your way?" The labor camp is to the southwest of Monroe, near the river. I want Clarice to stay off the narrow levee roads.
"There are a few people like me, heading toward Monroe. Oh..."
"What?" She may be whispering but I'm close to yelling.
"Ha!" Her voice is back to normal volume. "Some idiot just pulled out of a driveway between me and the SUV. He must've had to slam on his brakes. At least he's not right behind me now."
"How far out are you?"
"I'm only about eight miles away now and headed for the

freeway."

"OK, speed, drive a little erratically, don't get close to either shoulder and stay on your cell. In fact, keep it as visible possible. Take every chance you can to get a CHP to notice you."

I trip over a bag of melting frozen food on the way to my house phone and only put my cell down long enough to dial 911. When the dispatcher comes on I identify myself, ask for the Sheriff's duty officer and give him a rundown of Clarice's problem and location.

Then it's back to my cell. "Are you still there?"

"I'm here. I'm practically waving my cell phone out the window. Why is it when you want a cop, no one's around?"

"I've called 911 and dispatch said they'd send a car out. Head for the Sheriff's and pull in back. Whoever it is, I doubt they'll follow you to the department parking lot and there'll be plenty of people around. I'll meet you there."

I cram the barely-frozen stuff into the freezer, snap a leash on Mac and beat it for the garage. It's a fifteen minute drive to the sheriff's and I make it in eleven, whipping around the back of the building to find Clarice still waving her cell in the midst of three deputies.

She comes over at a race walk, pale and disheveled more than usual. I give her a brief hug and she bursts into tears. I've never seen her this upset.

"Did they follow you here?" I'm thinking a question might give her a chance to compose herself.

"I don't think so. I lost sight of them when I turned the corner onto Elm." The department fronts Elm Street so whoever it is, I doubt they saw her pull into the parking lot.

"Good. Have you made a report yet?" She's stopped crying but her eyes are wet, her nose has started to run so I dig in my purse and find a crumpled but clean tissue. She wipes, blows and nods thanks before she turns back to the clutch of deputies by her car.

"What I want to know is why nobody stopped me when I

was driving all over the road talking on my cell! Have you guys reached your ticket quota already?"

Boy, am I glad to see her back and, judging from their grins, the guys are, too. One of them waves her into the office to take her report and I hang around to figure out what the next best step is. Even with being scared, she's been observant and gives the deputy the make and model of the SUV, plus four digits of the California plate.

By the time we're finished, Mac is seriously pissed at being left in the car, but he cheers up at the sight of Clarice. A wet kiss and she's happier, too. "Well, this shot a hole in your night, Amy. I'm sorry."

"Oh, sorry, Clarice! That's bushwah. It's good you caught me and I got the deputies."

"Now what?"

That's a good question. "Let's leave your car here and we can go to my house. I'm going to ask for a deputy or a city cop to do some random drive-bys tonight. With the security I have and Mac, we should be fine. So far, whoever these guys are, they're just out to scare us."

If I say it out loud, it may make it true.

We pull together a dinner of chicken and vegetable skewers, salad and not-yet-stale French bread. Clarice clears up while I stash groceries and Mac roams between us, trying to decide whose bed he'll sleep on tonight.

#

This morning, I wake Clarice and drop her at her car before heading into work. There will be a report of last night on the log when she does her early cops check, but it's not worth a mention. What does get a mention is the call from Jim Dodson.

"Amy, it seems you and Clarice had some excitement last night."

"We did, Sheriff. She was a lot more alert than I was. I hope your guys will be able to use her information about the car."

I sense that Dodson is ticked at something. "Have you been able to track the SUV?" Maybe she didn't get enough to identify it.

"Even with the partial plate, we've managed to narrow it down to about fifty in the county. Of those, fifteen are registered to DiFazio Vineyards. It's what they use for field cars for their management." Dodson's voice sounds exasperated.

I can understand why he's ticked. He's going to have to take on one of the largest and most visible employers...one who has a national reputation in the high-end wine business and who's been rumored to be feeding donations to his possible campaign. This isn't making him a happy camper.

"Are you going to assign Clarice to do a story on this? It seems a little too early."

He's right, but not for all the right reasons. "It's too early, yes, but even then I couldn't assign Clarice. She's part of the story and not objective. If there's ever an arrest, someone else will have to cover it."

"Watch out for yourselves. These may be warnings and they may be attempts. The patrol guy said all was quiet at your house last night and they even swung by Clarice's apartment. No signs of anything there, either. I'll let you know if we find more."

Then a right-angle veer. "Is Clarice in yet?"

"Not yet. I'll have her call you."

Hmmm. He usually doesn't ask about her at work. Is he worried? Does he want to warn her too? Does he have more questions for her?

Head-slap, Amy. He probably wants to find our how to get her car to her. I do a sticky note in red marker and paste it on her screen.

She's sees it first thing and I watch the color ebb and wane while she talks to him. When she hangs up she had a dreamy look just long enough to catch my eye, then she bolts from her chair and is in my office before I can say "What?"

CHAPTER THIRTY-NINE

She closes my door behind her. "We have to talk."
"I think we are."
"No, I mean away from the office, away from the Sheriff. Can we do a late lunch? Can we leave early?"
I don't know what she and Dodson talked about, but something has stirred her up.
"We can leave early. Besides, we need to get your car. Or did the Sheriff have another idea for that?"
"Oh, that. He thinks I should leave it at the department for a few days. Or really, I can go over and use it for work, but leave it there at night. He said he'd have a deputy drive me home and pick me up."
That surprises me. The department always complains to the Board of Supervisors about how tight their budget is. There's a threat to cut back patrols in the sparsely populated rural areas of the county and that always sets up a howl from people who moved out of the city but still want all the city amenities.
She looks at me. "He told me that after I told him about the call."
"What call?"

"That's why I want to talk somewhere else. I had a message on my voice mail last night."

OK, then. We whip through some perfunctory things, I assign Steve to do cop calls this afternoon and evening, tell the copy editor that reads are his and we're out of there.

"Where do you suggest we go? It doesn't sound like either of our houses is secure."

"I'm out of ideas, Amy. Maybe a park?"

I don't relish the idea of sitting in a park in the afternoon heat, plus dust and bugs. "Let me call Nancy."

Nancy will be at work until seven tonight with the library's extended hours and says sure, use my house. She also says, "What's the hush-hush? What are you up to now? I know you won't tell until it's over, but you owe me a dinner and a lot of wine."

She's right about this hush-hush. I don't like it and from Clarice's expression, she doesn't like it either. She's pale and there's a hunted, deer-in-the-headlights look in her eyes. Plus she's got dark circles, telling me that even at my house she didn't sleep well.

Both of us have our eyes peeled behind us on the short drive. Nancy has even given me her garage door opener, so from the street there's no indication that anyone, let alone us, is home. I pour us both iced tea and we sit out on Nancy's covered patio.

"All right. What voicemail message?"

Clarice shakes her head. "It's time stamped at one-twenty-three this morning. Maybe he wanted to wake me up to scare me, but he left a message anyway. He said I was being watched. And I'd better tell the Sheriff, my boyfriend, that he was being watched, too. And my boss, that bitch from the newspaper, was working her way to the top of the list."

I'm speechless. Whoever this is, they're talking about hurting a lot of people.

"Who was it? Could you recognize a voice?"

"No. It's not anyone I know, didn't even sound familiar

enough that it may have been someone I've interviewed."

"It was a man?" She nods. "Did he have an accent?"

"Not really. There was a trace of something, as though he'd lived in the south for awhile, but it wasn't a true southern accent."

"Jesus, Clar, this is making me nervous."

"I know you've been attacked, but now I feel I'm the target. I wanted to talk to you about this and see if we can figure it out."

Lord, I don't know where to start. "Did Dodson tell you that the car is probably registered to DiFazio Vineyards?"

"He did."

"Well, that narrows down the suspects."

"I'm not so sure. The cars are for use by the management in vineyard operations, but I've seen the keys just hanging on a board in the receptionist's area."

"You mean anyone can walk in and grab a set?"

"No, there's more oversight than that. In order to get a set of keys, you have to check in with the receptionist, tell her where you're going and for how long, check the mileage when you leave then reverse the process when you get back. And only the chief financial officer, chief operating officer, grape supervisor, the chief technology officer, the vineyard supervisors and the DiFazios themselves are allowed to keep a car out overnight."

"So, we're being followed by some high-raking people."

She kicks her sandals off and looks in her iced tea, maybe hoping for some leaves to read. "That's if the system works right, Amy. Somebody could wait until the receptionist was gone and lift a set of keys. There are safeguards, but most of the employees who are allowed to check a car out have been with the DiFazios a long time. They're trusted. I don't think a big alarm would be raised if one car was gone overnight without being checked out."

"This doesn't eliminate many people. Did you get this information from Dodson?"

Now she looks sheepish. "No. And I didn't tell him either. I watched this the other day—my god, was it only yesterday?—when I was waiting to talk to people in *jefe's* office."

"The *jefe's* office is in the administration building?" That seemed odd. He had all the field crews in and out of his office and I didn't think the DiFazios would want them mingling with the grape brokers, winemasters and buyers who come to talk wine business.

"No. I checked in at admin so they knew I was there. The other day, I just found *jefe* in his office, but that made him really nervous so this time I thought I'd go through channels."

And what she did was alert all of the honchos at DeFazio to her presence. And someone took it a step farther and followed her.

She's watching my face and sees that I've figured that out. "Yep, Amy, in hindsight, I may as well have carried a big neon sign, 'Here I am, come and get me'. I wasn't very subtle."

I inhale, an ice cube starts down the wrong way and I'm choking and my eyes are streaming. Clarice leans over and pounds on my back. "You might think it's funny..." and she trails off, probably picturing a neon sign. "Well, I guess it is kinda funny."

"It's you, Clar, vintage you. You're good."

CHAPTER FORTY

"It just doesn't feel right." Clarice is trying to brush back the hair falling in her eyes. She's overdue for a trim and will probably take scissors to it herself rather than trying to get an appointment. I set her up with my stylist once...and it was only once. "Jeez, Amy, she charged me seventy-five dollars! And she said that was her friend rate! I don't ever want to see her enemy rate!"

"What doesn't feel right?" I'm daydreaming about Clarice getting a make-over.

"The whole drugs thing. Sure, we have workers coming up from Mexico. And we have our own meth labs. And I'll bet we have grow houses in some of those new housing developments but we're not in the middle of any major routes either north-south or east-west."

She's hit on something I hadn't thought of and she has a point. There are warehousing companies going in around us—on the I-5, I-80 and I-205 corridors, the main east-west and north-south routes. I-5 runs from Tijuana to the Canadian border and I-80 is the northern route across the country. Would traffickers need to be near those hubs? On the other hand, they're probably not transporting their drugs in semis, so maybe the interstate system isn't important.

"I don't know, Clar. There're huge profits in small amounts of drugs, particularly coke and heroin. I think they use regular cars or pickups. It wouldn't matter that we're not right on a major highway. In fact, it could be a diversion."

She's mulling it over and absently tugging on her hair. "But if they stuck to the interstates for most of their distribution, they'd have fewer jurisdictions to deal with. If you're carrying a load of heroin for the Mexican Mafia, you sure don't want to be stopped for some traffic infraction by the Podunk cops."

I sip on my tea, now diluted to a pale tan and tasteless. We are speculating. There isn't enough information either to pin the murders on drugs or to rule drugs out. I have a twinge of empathy for Jim Dodson, having all those feds around trying to find connections.

As my mind spins merrily along, a piece from the back of my head comes up to smack me. "We never really talked about your last visit to the camp. Besides being scared out of your wits at the tail and noticing the keys hanging on the board, what did you find out?"

"Oh." She looks startled. "There was agreement that neither of the field workers were using heroin. Everybody was adamant on that. The truck driver used to hang out with the *jefe* and they'd watch the gondolas get filled. Four of the field workers had dates with Angel the night she was killed, plus jefe got his blow job..." She's quiet a minute, then says, "Did they swab Angel for any DNA samples?"

"I don't know. I didn't think about it because she was a hooker so I assumed there'd be so much semen that it'd be meaningless. I'll call Dodson."

"Don't bet on it. I'm sure she had them all use condoms."

While I'm on the phone Clarice gets more tea for us and has even raided Nancy's pantry for some chips. She gives me a funny look. "Do you think Nancy will mind?"

"It's a little after the fact, but no, I don't think so. They did swab for DNA and found two different samples. I thought you said she'd had four customers."

"Well, there's that condom thing. I'm kinda surprised they found any. Have they matched anyone yet?"

I shook my head. "No they're still collecting cheek swabs. A couple of the field workers balked and the *jefe* didn't want to donate, either. He said he only had a blow job so they said they'd swabbed Angel's mouth as well and the test could rule him out as well as in, so he agreed. She probably used a condom for those as well, but this is all just guesses. And even if they do find matches, so what? She was a hooker and she had sex."

"I know. I really don't like us going down this path. After I met Samuel Bonham and heard Jesse's story, my idea of her changed. She was a woman who had demons and she fought them the best way she knew how."

"Anything else you heard at the camp?"

"No, well a couple of the guys said they'd heard complaints about the way the vines were being harvested."

This was an area where I had some knowledge. "What do you mean? Either they're hand-harvested or by machine."

"I don't mean physically how, I mean the order that they were using. You'd think they'd just go up one row and down the next, but they were skipping all over the vineyard—a row here, a row there then back to the first part. The guys said they couldn't set up and keep a rhythm. That means a lot when they get paid by the picked pound."

I nodded. It sounded odd, but I'd learned that Zins ripen at different rates and you could have ripe, high sugar berries in the same bunch as less ripe, greener ones. And the sugar makes the alcohol.

"We're back where we started. What does any of this have to do with drugs?"

Clarice gazes across Nancy's yard. Is she hunting squirrels? "I can't get my mind around drugs. There's not enough to convince me that major drug deals are going down. I think I would have heard something over the past few months. And even the cops and the sheriff's department haven't said anything. They'd be the first to crow if they got a big bust. That's the kind of publicity that looks good and let's them keep their budgets."

"I agree, and think you're right. But if it's not drugs, what is it?"

She's come back from her squirrel hunt. "It could be something as simple as jealousy. Both of the workers had the hots for Angel..."

"Wait a minute! I find it hard to buy that field workers are in love with a prostitute."

"Amy, these are guys who leave home for months at a time, who do heavy, nasty, hot manual labor so we can have our cheap food and expensive wine, they can't bring their wives or girlfriends. Then this woman shows up and she's nice to them. Everybody knows her, everybody likes her. It may not be what we think of as a love interest, but it could work for them."

I'm abashed. Have I put my white middle-class sensibilities and suppositions out there and decided these men didn't deserve love? Or that my ideas about love were the only correct ones? Now *I* look for the squirrel.

"You're right. It could be something as simple as jealousy, as a love triangle. But how does that explain Angel?"

"You're saying 'triangle'. How do we know there were only two guys involved? It could be that the murderer was in love with her and killed off some of the opposition, but she kept seeing men and the old 'If I can't have her exclusively, then nobody can' syndrome kicked in. Women have been murdered for a lot less."

This has been an interesting afternoon, I've enjoyed tossing around ideas with Clarice, but at the end, we're iced-tea logged and no closer to any answers. In fact we've added a couple more questions.

I take her back to the Sheriff's department where she'll get a ride home. I could take her home, but I think it's a good idea that whoever the bad guys are, they see both of us being watched out for by law enforcement. It won't stop a really determined person, but if their threats and "incidents" are scare tactics, it may make them back off.

I think that until I'm home and reach into my mailbox. There's an unmailed post card with "Your dog is next" scrawled in black marker.

CHAPTER FORTY-ONE

My hands are shaking as I hit the garage door opener. Everything looks fine and normal, but I stay in the car until the door fully closes. I go in through the laundry room and Mac is there, squirming and jumping with his, "Oh good, you're home! Let's go, let's go," routine.

I drop my purse, keys and phone and collapse in a heap on the floor, needing to hold him and hug him. He doesn't understand, but as long as I'm home, he'll put up with it.

It's still light out so I change in a hurry and snap on his leash for a walk. I hope Mr. Juarez is out with the Schnauzers tonight. I'll ask him if he saw anyone putting something in my mailbox. He is out, the Schnauzers bark then fall all over themselves saying hello and he saw nothing out of the ordinary today.

Home, I head for the kitchen and notice the blinking red light. Now what? Heather needing more money? I hit the play button and am pulling salad things out of the fridge when a man's voice says, "Hello, Amy. I see you're not home yet or you're screening your calls. No matter, I'll call Heather in Santa Barbara."

A head of butter lettuce hits the floor, followed by an egg.

I can't scream. I can barely breathe. I sink to the floor with my head between my knees. Mac is interested but can't decide whether the novelty of seeing me on the floor twice in one night is a higher priority than a smashed egg.

I manage to get up and grab the phone, hit Heather's speed dial number and when she answers I burst into tears.

"Mom, Mom is that you? What's going on?"

"Oh honey, I'm so glad to hear your voice." I know mine is shaky. I take a deep breath and will my hands to be still.

"Have you gotten any strange phone calls? From men whose voice you don't recognize?"

"No, Mom! What's the matter?"

"Are you sure one of your roommates hasn't answered a call?"

"Mom, we all have cell phones. Only a few calls come to the house phone, and we screen those. If we don't recognize the number, it doesn't get answered."

I wonder if it's safer not to hear a threat, then I fill Heather in. Just the skeleton, enough for her to be wary but not enough to cause panic.

"M-o-t-h-e-r." Uh-oh When she calls me that, and in that suffering tone, I'm in trouble. "Mother, this is serious! You were in a hit-and-run."

"I know, but I get threats all the time. I've never had anyone say they'll call you. Please be careful, don't go anywhere alone." Who am I kidding? Heather *never* goes anywhere alone.

"Do you want me to come home?"

That's a nice offer and she's definitely worried. "No sweetie. You'd lose your job and then whoever the bad guys are would have both of us in the same place. Not a good idea. Stay put, stay alert and call me. I love you."

By the time I hang up, my panic is overridden by anger. Who are these scum, these...I run through every curse I know and make some up. How dare they threaten my daughter and my dog?

Jim Dodson gave me his cell number when he was here and I call it now. When he answers I run through tonight's threats.

"Amy, this is escalating. We need to share this with the task force."

"Please, no, Jim. I don't want Skies having any more information about me than he already has. I would appreciate it if you'd call both the Santa Barbara and the UC police and tell them that Heather is being used as a threat."

"Of course. Do you want me to ask them to do a welfare check?"

"No, I just talked to her and it's calm down there. No calls on either her cell or her home phone. I've told her the basics, but I didn't tell her that I was going to ask the cops to check on her. I'd like them to be alerted in case she's approached."

There's silence on the other end and I think the call's dropped when he says, "I'm going to call Jack and see how your gun sale is coming. And I'm calling the Monroe PD with this and ask for more random drive-bys."

Normally, I don't panic. Between being Vinnie's widow and the rash of nastiness I get over our coverage, most things roll off my back. Right now, I'm grateful and happy that someone else is helping look after me.

As I clean up the kitchen mess and start some dinner again, I debate calling Phil. Is it him I miss or do I just need a friendly voice on the phone? We've known each other for so long that it feels comfortable talking to him about anything.

But that was then. Now, does our intimate relationship change the dynamics? If I call him because of fear, will he think I expect him to rescue me? Or if he offers help and I turn him down, will he think I'm brushing him off?

This is giving me a headache. I eat my salad with CNN as background and am giving the kitchen a final clean when the house phone rings.

I jump, then edge over to check the caller ID. Not sure why I'm so edgy. The phone itself can't hurt me and I can always let it go to voice mail. Just as the message starts I see it's Phil's number and grab it. "Don't hang up! I'm here."

"I'm glad for that!" His voice teeters on a laugh. "What was that all about?"

"Are you using your ESP? I was thinking about calling you."

"ESP? I didn't know I had it. What were you going to call me about?"

And it all comes out in a rush; Clarice's tail, the threat to Mac, the veiled threat to Heather.

"Wait, Amy, are you home now?" His voice isn't teasing now, it has deep concern.

"I'm home. I called the Sheriff and reported it. He's going to call the Monroe police and have some officers drive by tonight. He's also calling the gun shop to see if my clearance has come through."

"Gun? You're buying a gun?"

Oops, I hadn't mentioned that to Phil. It's not that I hid it. In hindsight, if he's going to be spending time at my house, he should probably know there's a gun here.

"I asked the Sheriff to help me. He agreed and I've taken a couple of lessons."

He blows out a breath. "I can see there're changes at *Maison* Hobbes. Are you still taking overnight guests?"

"No, Clarice is staying at..." Duh, he's not asking about Clarice. I start again. "There are still a few people who have invitations, yes. Why do you ask?"

"Remember I told you about the loaned exhibition? The curating teams are meeting this Friday, tomorrow, and I'm coming over to sit in. I thought I'd stay a couple of nights, if you'll have me."

Have him? It will be wonderful to share time and maybe even my fears with someone who'd seen me through the most traumatic event in my life. When Vinnie was killed, Phil was unobtrusive, letting me know he was there to talk any time I needed it. And if I hadn't met Brandon, maybe Phil and I would have gotten together then. Our past is littered with bad timing. This may make up for that and I wanted to be sure that I was open with him.

"Yes, I'll have you. I'd love to see you. What time will you be here?"

"Not sure. I'll call you as soon as the meeting breaks up. In the meantime, stay safe and put the Sheriff's number on speed-dial! *A bientot!*"

CHAPTER FORTY-TWO

Jim Dodson calls me Friday morning to tell me my gun is ready.

Suddenly I have chills.

When this was a discussion, an exercise in learning to shoot, it was academic. Now I'm actually going to go pick up a Glock and take it home. Should I back out?

No. This was something Vinnie wanted me to do years ago. I got rid of his guns after he was killed because the sight of them brought him back. I'll always remember him, I'll always miss and care for him, but I had to close that chapter and move on with my life, both for me and for Heather. This feels right even though I haven't thought about a gun for years.

I spend a few minutes with Clarice, filling her in on the threats. I hadn't wanted to call her at home, it felt like I was dumping my fears on her and she was worried enough. Her reaction is a mix of anger and fear.

"Who are these jerks! Threatening Mac? I want to punch them out for that. And calling Heather! That's just sick. I wonder if they pulled the wings off flies and killed cats when they were kids!"

When I tell her about my conversation with Dodson she gets a tinge of pink. "That's good! He'll figure this out. He's way better at this than those feds." She practically spits "feds" out as though it's left a nasty taste. I have to agree with her.

Then I tell her about the trip to Jack's Gun Shop with Dodson and that Phil is coming over later today. Her mouth is an O. I'm not sure if she's surprised, jealous or angry, thinking I'm stepping into her personal territory.

"Shut your mouth, Clarice. This first is strictly business and the second is not your business. I'll call you later."

Jack's takes longer than I anticipate. Jack and Dodson want to make sure I'm able to fill the magazines and load them, that I can flick the safety off with one hand, that I can hold the gun steady and hit what I aim at—at least close to what I aim at. I'm hitting the target every time, not necessarily the bulls-eye—and that I know how to clean it.

We walk out with the gun a cleaning kit and a box of bullets.

I tell Dodson that my friend Phil is coming over from San Francisco to spend the weekend. He approves. He and Phil met earlier when a shady art dealer was after a stolen piece of art hidden for sixty years in an historic hotel in the Sierra foothills. The last time they'd seen each other was when they picked me up from the hospital after that little "incident".

I suddenly have a flash of...maybe not inspiration, maybe meddling...and say, "Are you doing anything later this evening? I'd like to invite you over for a glass of wine. And maybe I'll ask Clarice if she's free. It might be good to talk about some of this in a relaxed setting."

"I'm available. If you ask Clarice, call me and I'll pick her up. We're still keeping her car over night at the department lot."

Well, look at this! I haven't been a hostess since Brandon took off with his pregnant girlfriend. I need to get home, put the gun away, make a list and run to the store. I call Clarice and tell her the plan, call Dodson and tell him she'll be ready about nine, call Phil and tell him the change in plans while I'm choosing a pork tenderloin to grill with nectarines, spinach and strawberries for a salad and Yukon gold potatoes. Also some Brie and crackers.

Call Phil back and ask if he'll choose some wine. You'd think I'd asked him to judge the Miss America pageant, he says yes before I finished the sentence.

He cuts out of his meeting early and by a little after five we're having drinks out by the pool. The evening holds traces of warmth but clouds have gathered, drifting down from the northern Pacific. They're a harbinger of fall rains. For tonight they give a beautiful flamingo, peach, tangerine, lilac and turquoise show as the sun sets.

While there's still some light, we take Mac for a walk and I introduce Phil to the Schnauzers and Mr. Juarez. "You're the one who saw Amy's accident," Phil says.

"Accident! That was no accident." Mr. Juarez is angry all over again. "That sonofagun must have headed directly for her and then when she was in the air, he took off! That was deliberate and I'd sure like to get my hands on whoever was driving."

Phil nods. "I agree it was deliberate. Thanks to you she got medical attention right away." He looks over at me. "And for that, I want to thank you."

Mr. Juarez looks back and forth between us, makes a small noise and smiles. I can hear him thinking "So that's the way it is..."

Home again, Phil claims the barbecue duties while I shred spinach and slice strawberries. We eat by the pool lights and candles and talk is just talk. A lot of "Do you remember?" and "Have you seen?" which gives me a warm rush for our companionship.

As we're cleaning up, Phil asks me about Clarice and Dodson.

"I don't know, exactly. I try to keep Clarice's personal life out of our relationship at work. I have talked to her about

Vinnie and me and about the pitfalls of getting involved with your sources. Not to mention getting hooked up with a cop. When you have two adrenaline junkies together, it's not calm and serene."

He's getting out some wine glasses. "How does he feel about her? If he breaks it off, you'll have to pick up the pieces."

"I don't know if it's gotten far enough to have a break-up." I'm leaning back against the sink eyeing Phil. Is this really a Q and A about Clarice and Jim Dodson or is there some underlying tenor about Phil and Amy? Let it go, Amy. I have enough on my plate with someone after me. Not a good idea to throw some "how does he feel" free-ranging emotions into the mix.

As we start to lay out wine, cheese, crackers, napkins, fancy plates that haven't seen the light of day for several years, the gun pops into my head. Maybe it's a subliminal wish to shoot Brandon...or maybe not. I know I'm way better off without him.

"I told you I bought a gun?"

"You did. I'm surprised. Do you have it?"

I take him upstairs. I've put the gun in my bedside table for now and the box of bullets on the shelf in my closet. He picks it up, makes sure the safety is on and ejects the magazine.

I'm standing there, my jaw on my chest.

"I didn't know you knew anything about guns! Have you used one before?"

He grins at me. "You can ask me that after seeing the cutthroat art world? Yes, I did have one once. Living in LA and working in a business where what I wrote affected someone's ability to make enough money to feed themselves? Almost all journalists get some sort of threats, but I thought one guy in particular would follow through. I bought a gun and even took shooting lessons."

"What happened?" This is a side of Phil that I've never seen.

"After three years, the guy gave up his so-called career and went to work for his dad's car dealership. Last I heard he was making more than a hundred thou and mixing with minor celebs. You probably should find a better place to keep this and the ammo. If you have a burglary—and the way your life's been going that's a probability—these are the first places the burglar will look."

"What happened to the gun? Do you still have it?"

"No, I threw it in the LA river."

He's choking with laughter at my expression of horror.

"I sold it back to the gun shop where I bought it."

CHAPTER FORTY-THREE

Saved by the bell.
Mac sets up a barking spree. "Somebody's here! Somebody's at the door! Maybe they'll pet me! Do I get another walk? Am I protecting you?"
Clarice and Jim Dodson are all smiles as they come in, hers nervous, his calm.
"Hi, you remember Phil Etange, don't you?" I ask as I close the door behind them.
Phil steps forward, shakes Dodson's hand, gives Clarice a quick hug and cheek-kiss and says "Good to see both of you again. At least this time Amy's not in the hospital."
Everybody chuckles and we move into the family room. Phil asks "White or red?", we sort ourselves out with drinks and snacks at hand and...silence descends.
Clarice leans over to rub Mac's ears, Dodson asks Phil how his drive over was, I take a big slug of white—interesting, it's a Sauvignon Blanc from New Zealand—and clear my throat. We need to talk about the elephant.
"I've told Phil most of what's been happening. I thought it would be good if we could put our heads together. As you know, Sheriff" and I turn to Dodson, "I don't have much

faith in the feds theory about drugs."

"Call me Jim, please. Sherriff is my job, not who I am. I think I agree with you, Amy. There's no doubt there are drugs here, but I just can't see Monroe as the center of a big drug territory."

Phil leans over for a cracker. "Amy hasn't given me the details. How were Angel and the field workers killed? Did you find a murder weapon yet?"

"All three of them had been slashed with a grape knife, a sharp hooked blade for pulling the bunches to you and cutting them off during harvest. We took all the ones we found in for testing. The tool examiner couldn't pin any one specifically as the weapon. There were traces of blood on several. Those are sharp and the workers occasionally cut themselves, so just blood doesn't mean anything. What blood we swabbed didn't match either of the field workers or Angel."

He suddenly looks at Clarice. "You know that this whole conversation is off the record, right?"

Her face takes on the color of the red wine she's drinking. "Yes, of course I know that Sher...uh, Jim."

Is she embarrassed that he said that, or that he's talking to her in front of people? She slides back on the couch and her eyes drill into the back of his head. OK, she's pissed he pointed out this wasn't anything she could use.

Phil rescues. "I suspect you guys know most of this already, but it's good of you to recap, Jim. Have persons of interest?"

"Only most of the labor camp and now the administration of DiFazio Vineyards. Another field worker may have done the slicing but he wasn't driving a company car that ran Amy down and followed Clarice."

"This is sounding like a real whodunit. No weapon, no witnesses, hours of opportunity. Have you found who profits?" I wonder how many cop TV shows Phil's been watching.

"Amy and I were talking about that yesterday." Clarice has

scooted forward again and is engaging herself in the conversation. "We have maybe three different motives. Whoever, if anyone, is running the drugs through the camp. Plain old jealousy and perverted sense of ownership of Angel, and something hinky about the grapes themselves."

She's succinctly laid out our best three ideas.

"Jealousy? We haven't given that one much thought." Jim twirls his glass. "That seems a little far-fetched to be jealous as of a prostitute's affections. The other two..."

"I don't think it's that far-fetched." Clarice came up with the jealousy motive and she's defending it. "She runs through her "lonely guys away from home" speech, adds some Friday night beer to the scenario and smugly crossed her arms.

Dodson looks at her speculatively. "I think that's the right underpinning for the few fights and stabbings we get during harvest but in this case it doesn't answer why someone from DiFazio has made you and Amy targets. The field workers don't have access to the SUVs; they wouldn't be out driving around at night, they're way too tired, and harming either of you wouldn't do them any good."

There is that. I watch as Clarice deflates like a leaky balloon. "Well then, what are we left with?"

"The top place contenders are drugs and grapes. What are the benefits and drawbacks?" I feel like a teacher or seminar leader. "Drugs. We have no indication that Monroe is or has been a hub of drug activity. Most of the drugs on the West Coast—well, other than our homegrown ones—come through Mexico. They're funneled through and handled by the LA gangs and dealers. Those guys have their distribution networks set up and I think we're just too small, too far off the major tracks, to be of interest."

"We're just not an easy distribution center." Clarice looks pleased as she voices her theory.

"The benefits to drugs are pretty clear." Phil is counting off on his fingers. "Money, money, money, fear, more money, large pool to recruit from, money." I smile as he waggles three fingers to come up with a full set of ten reasons.

"Grapes, on the other hand..." he realizes he's almost out of hands so he starts over with the fingers. "Money, money, prestige, honors, money, increasing assets, growth, money."

"Gee, does it seem possible that greed could be a motive for either of these?"

This time, we laugh and it's good, it breaks the tension.

"Thanks, Phil. If you ever get laid-off at the *Times* or get tired of journalism, come on by and we can talk about a job. You have such a probing mind." Jim's looking relaxed. "The catch is that greed only narrows our suspects down by about half."

"Amy's been doing some research on grapes," Phil motions to me. Does he have a proud look? "There's definitely a profit motive here."

I nod. "Depending on the grape and the volume, there could be a million dollars or more every year from substituting red table wine grapes for premium varietals."

Jim says, "But who would ever know? The winery? The customer?"

"I doubt the average customer would notice much difference." Phil gets up to bring the bottles to the table. "If a bottle didn't have any of the grapes it says it does—in other words if this Pinot Noir has no Pinot grapes in it—we'd know. But would the average person know if ten percent or twenty percent were another red grape? Probably not. And that could save the winery a lot of money every year. Money that could get kicked back to the winemaster, the shipper, the broker, the grower."

"This is the crux of it." Jim looks tired and stressed now. "With either of these, we have a potful of suspects, a host of people involved and a few making money all the way up the line. Ultimately, whoever's at the top makes the most and has a motive to kill. Sorting it out like this doesn't get us any closer to the right answer."

We all nod our agreement and Phil deftly moves the

conversation to what he's discovered in the Delta. Both Clarice and Jim add their suggestions about their favorite spots and Clarice asks what we have planned for tomorrow.

I start a snippy comment then realize she's just making small talk. "I don't know. Phil's such a wine buff that we may go look at some the vineyards or do some tasting." I glance over at Phil. "We haven't talked about it yet."

With a smile, Phil says "Amy's right, but I haven't got a burning agenda. Just letting the day unfold is fine with me."

CHAPTER FORTY-FOUR

It feels as though we're a married couple as we pick up glasses and dishes, turn out the lights, give Mac a last outdoor visit and head upstairs.

I'm taking off my shirt when Phil comes up behind me and begins nuzzling my neck and nips at my earlobe. A shiver runs down my back and I shake myself like a wet dog. "If you keep that up you're going to find out..."

"Find out what?" he says as he turns me around.

"This." I press myself against his chest and start to kiss and lick his lips. He suddenly pulls my head back and kisses me deeply, moving his tongue inside my mouth and waking up every bit of me.

Afterward, I'm lying on his chest dozing off when he says, "It'd really a shame..."

"What's a shame? Making love with you certainly isn't a shame and caring..."

His chest is making funny sounds. Then I realize he's laughing. I sit up and smack him with a pillow. "What's a shame?"

"Before you got all huffy, I started to say it's a shame we couldn't arrest and convict someone on a consensus. I think all of us tonight agreed on greed and that grapes were in the lead."

I lie back down in the crook of his shoulder, his arm comforting me around my healing ribcage. "I think we're right, but that doesn't get us to a killer, a weapon, an opportunity. This must be hard on Jim, his gut telling him to look for the murderer in the DiFazio management, the DEA telling him to look for drugs among the field workers. It's clear that some facet of the DiFazios is involved. And however that shakes out, this town is going to be shocked to its roots.

"Oh, my God!" I bolt upright, practically dragging Phil's arm with me.

"What? This better be good. I think you've dislocated my shoulder. Ow!"

Now he's up, rubbing his shoulder and giving me a fish eye.

"Remember I told you about the chamber guy?"

"What chamber guy? You mean that sleeze I met at the crush party?"

"Yes. John Nesman. Did I tell you about my conversation with him?"

"I have no recollection of it."

Great, he's giving me the favorite trial attorney answer, neither a "yes" nor a "no".

"I called him before I went over to talk to the UC Davis people. He was chilly but when he began talking about the economic impact of wines and vines on Monroe he was as passionate as I've ever heard him. Then when I mentioned Davis there was a silence before he asked why I was going there. And when he hung up, I thought I heard another click, as though someone else had been listening."

Phil is silent, then he says, "We'll he's right about the economic impact on Monroe and on Madison County. DiFazio hires a lot of people directly and another group benefits indirectly. Retail, automotive, all the service businesses."

"I don't know. An awful lot of the workers are migrants. They may spend some money here but they don't use services—well, there was Angel, but she was pretty underground. They don't earn much and they spend money primarily on food and beer."

"Beyond the field workers," Phil's voice is patient, as if he's explaining things to a third-grader, "there are quite a few well-paying jobs at DeFazio. All the administrative employees, the contract workers who come in for the testings, the contracts with the brokers, I'm sure that DeFazio is the economic engine for this area. And nobody, most of all the head of the Chamber of Commerce, would want to see anything damage that. "

He's right, of course. And I think I know this but wasn't letting it come to the top. If DiFazio folds, people in Monroe will be hurt, the retail businesses will be hurt, the *Press'* advertising will be hurt and even I can be hurt, losing my job.

This isn't a happy scenario. On the other hand, if there is fraud going on at the vineyard, and people had been killed to hush it up, law enforcement needs to find the killer or killers and we need to cover the story.

Jim, Phil, Clarice and I may have agreed that it's more likely a killer is in the vines, but a nasty drug capo from Mexico or LA is a lot cleaner and less disruptive to the town's well-being.

I dream of grape knives, needles, bottles of wine and wake to the smell of coffee. Even in my house, Phil is a take-charge guy when it comes to mornings, a nice balance to my snaillike movements just to get my eyes open. I manage a quick brush of teeth and hair and a clean t-shirt and shorts before I trot downstairs.

He's sitting at the kitchen island, reading the *Press* with his laptop open to the *Times* online version while CNN is muted during a commercial. And I thought *I* was a news junkie! When he hears me, he looks over, smiles and waves at a cup next to the pot. "I didn't pour yours. I didn't want it to get cold."

Is this a very considerate action or a snide comment that I stayed in bed longer than he did? Way too much to try to out-guess for the morning, so I just kiss his cheek and say thanks.

"What are your, or our, plans for today?" I don't have an agenda, there's no right or wrong answer to this question, it's information gathering, good to know so I'll have clothes or anything else I need ready.

"I liked your wine tasting idea, not that we need to drink much wine." Phil closes his laptop. "There are several boutique wineries in Amador County and Lodi is getting attention. I would like to take you to diner tonight, though. I heard about a nice restaurant in Sacramento, if that's not too far to drive. The curators were talking about it yesterday."

I grab my coffee and head for the shower, telling Phil there's raspberry coffee ring in the fridge. When I come back to the kitchen, he's warmed it in the microwave and has a fresh pot of coffee.

The day is perfect. It's the tail of Indian summer, warm with a hint of cool to come. We take Phil's Porsche so he can give her a taste of the mountain roads. These aren't narrow like the Delta ones, but wind lazily along the rise of the foothills where grazing cattle and Valley oaks give way to brush and pine.

We stop at two small wineries, ask some tourist questions, try a couple of whites and head out again. A late lunch at a sidewalk cafe in Sutter Creek and we head back to my house.

"Why don't you pull your car in the garage? I should have thought about it last night." I didn't. It may have felt too familiar.

Phil looks at me and says OK. He has a funny almost-smile tugging at the corner of his mouth.

I dump my purse at the end of the kitchen island and open the doors to the patio. Mac goes boiling out to look for trespassers and only finds a squirrel, standing on the crossbar of the fence and chittering, undoubtedly four-letter squirrel words. I can hear Phil's voice on the phone and then he's calling , "Amy, Amy?"

"In the back," I yell.

"I didn't know how hungry you'd be, but I made a reservation for eight o'clock at Enotria."

"Ohh, that's supposed to be a good restaurant! And, oh, duh, should have thought of this, it's even been given an award for it's wine selection. Great choice."

I put my arms around his waist and lean into his chest while he strokes my hair. "I've enjoyed today and I have high hopes for tonight," he purrs in my ear.

CHAPTER FORTY-FIVE

I have a couple of dresses in mind for tonight. While I go upstairs to make the final choice, Phil offers to take Mac for his evening walk. "I could use the exercise," he says, "and it will give us some man-to-man bonding time." What does that mean? Is Phil planning to become a fixture in Mac's life...and by extension, in mine?

Whatever, I have more important things right now. Like what shoes to wear. I can wear heels with Phil and the slingback red ones make me feel sexy. With Phil around, I really don't need the shoes for that, though.

They'll be good with a striped red and white silk dress, a white jacket and a red scarf. I dig through a couple of drawers and finally find the scarf balled up in the back of one. When I pull it out, it needs pressing. I head for the kitchen, pull out the ironing board and plug the iron in, running through what jewelry I can wear.

The iron is in my hand quietly steaming when suddenly I can't breathe. Somebody or something has grabbed me around the throat. With my free hand I try and pull loose but the grip is tightened.

"Don't struggle." The voice is rough and low. Is there a

trace of an accent?

"We're getting sick of you and your little pal. You keep poking around. We told you to back off. You didn't listen."

I'm trying to squirm away from the arm when it suddenly slides down and wraps around my still-bruised ribs. I gasp at the pain that shoots around my chest and radiates up my back.

"Found one of the spots from the accident, didn't I? Well this time it's gonna hurt more and gonna be permanent."

"Who are you?" My voice is raspy from being choked. "What do you want?"

Now the voice is hissing in my ear and his breath reeks of beer. "What's the matter with you? We're serious."

"What did you do, drink a case of beer to get your courage up to attack a woman?"

Oops, now I've made him mad and he jerks even tighter. My ribs are screaming in pain and I let out a moan. If I can force myself to relax, he may loosen his grip but I don't think I have a chance of pulling away from him. I have a fleeting thought of my gun...safe upstairs and too far to be a help.

This is the final irony, I break down and buy a gun for protection and when I need it, it's not there.

Think, think! One heavy, strong arm is pressing against my ribs, smashing me into a thick body. Is there a shirt on the arm? I move my elbow toward me and touch flesh, not my own. And his face...stubble is rasping at my ear. He's not wearing a mask.

I force myself to go limp, all the while my ribs shouting at me, "Don't move!" The arm has more weight on it now as it's helping hold me up as well as keeping me pinned, but this is what I want, having his muscles flexed.

Ignoring the signals from my ribs, I lift my right hand and swing it, with the steaming iron, flat against the arm and hold it there.

He lets out a terrible scream and pushes me and the iron away so hard I fall over the ironing board. I catch myself on the counter before I hit the floor, whirl around and smack the iron into his cheek.

I hear something clatter and look down. He has a knife but he's dropped it because he's trying to hold up his burnt arm. I stare at it a second. I know I know what it is, but it's not coming to me.

"You bitch! You stinking bitch! I told them we should have gotten rid of you!"

He's trying to get to the faucet and I get my first good look at him. I have no idea who he is, I've never seen him before.

That's when a voice behind me says, "Hey, all right! Hold it right there! I have gun."

I'm immobilized. Attacked in my own kitchen and then shot dead. Jeez, there isn't any story that's worth this. I don't move, but my brain unfreezes enough to let a few facts in, among them that I know that voice.

"Phil?"

"Yeah, it's me. Move away from him, fast!"

He sure doesn't have to tell me twice, I scramble around the end of the island and behind him, telling my ribs to shut up.

"Who are you?" I ask. Phil glances at me in wonder. "You mean someone comes into your house, attacks you and you don't know him?"

"He kept saying 'we' so I'm pretty sure he's with the DiFazios, but I don't know where he fits in."

The man is now moaning in pain, trying to get his burnt arm under the cold water faucet and his face is squinched up in pain from the burn on his cheek.

"Careful. You, buster, don't move. Amy, go back and get that knife and kick it out of his reach. Then use the house phone to call 911 so they can patch in your address."

All done. Then I get a good look at the knife. It's a grape knife, the kind with a hook on the end, a knife identical to the one that slit the throats of two field workers and Angel.

"Who are you?"

"Jorge Felix."

"Who? I've never heard your name before."
"Most of the time I'm called *jefe*."

CHAPTER FORTY-SIX

We never make our reservation at Enotria.
All the first responders responded, with the added attraction of Sheriff Jim Dodson.
It was in the city limits so the Monroe Police Department took Felix into custody, keeping him under watch until he was treated for his burns, only first degree, unfortunately. He rode in the ambulance with a cop escort.
I got looked at by the paramedics, again, and this time they suggested I could get to the hospital by myself for precautionary X-rays.
Phil and Jim had a great chat, pleased with themselves that they'd identified grapes as the motive behind the murders.
Clarice showed up as Felix was being loaded into the ambulance and gave him a look that could freeze his bone marrow. She didn't dare say anything but I was pretty sure I could hear her saying every Spanish cuss word she knew under her breath. What I could hear was, "you pig!"
Now, on Sunday morning, Phil and I are back to our couple role, hosting a brunch for Clarice and Jim Dodson. We have to eat, but both of us secretly want to know what Felix' statement is and how this fits together. And Clarice is sporting

ears like a Bassett, trying to take it all in and still steamed at the treachery of the *jefe*.

It doesn't come out in a smooth narrative. I heard Phil's part last night as we came home from the hospital. My ribs are still cracked but healing and it's rest, ice and no sudden twists, so Phil had me ensconced in bed, propped up with pillows, my phone, laptop, book and smoothie on a jerry-rigged table across the bed. He'd carved out a small spot for himself too, but said he'd sleep in the guest room and I was tired enough that I didn't argue.

He had taken Mac for a walk. When he got back to the house, he found a DiFazio SUV parked in the driveway. He figured this wasn't a social call, so he wrapped Mac's leash around the neighbor's mailbox and tried the front door. It was unlocked. He came in quietly, peeked around the door into the kitchen and saw Felix with a death grip on my ribs. He went upstairs, got the Glock and came back down, just in time to see me smash the iron into Felix's face.

"Boy, I wondered why you'd even bought a gun after seeing that," he said. "Remind me never to cross you when you have an iron in your hand. Do you iron often, by the way?"

I started to laugh, hugged my ribs and grinned. "Not often."

After all the furor, and poor Mac barking his head off until the neighbor came out to shout at him, Phil had smoothed things over, put Mac in the back yard with some food, loaded me in my car and driven to the hospital. The ER was alerted I was coming in only for X-rays and they were in a dither. Saturday night was usually their busiest, but they didn't often get a patient complete with a police guard.

We take coffee, juice, Danish and a bowl of fruit salad out to the umbrella table by the pool and settle in for the rehash, putting all our facts together to make a whole. Clearly, Jim has the most information. We eye-pin him to the chair until he begins.

"All right. Well, all, right, we were looking at the murderer being from the labor camp and we were sure it wasn't drug related, but it did set us back when heroin was found in the workers' tox screens. By that time, Skies, the DEA and FBI agents were full-cry after a smuggling link. We never found any traceable DNA on the knives and machetes so we had to work the motive instead of a suspect."

Clarice starts with, "I told you we had motives. You guys all made fun of me when I brought up jealousy..."

"I know Clar," I begin. "I've known you long enough not to just reject any of your ideas or feelings. The trouble is when we ended up with notes on our cars it was something way bigger that a love triangle...or rectangle."

Clarice scoots her chair a smidge to the left, getting out of the sun. Even this late in the year, her fair skin can't take much. The move also narrows the distance between her and Jim. My dark glasses hide my small frown. I wonder...

"The notes were non-specific enough that it still could have been either drugs or fraudulent grape deals. Like you two, though, I just didn't see the types and volume of drugs that Skies was talking about." Dodson puts a piece of Danish and some salad on his plate. "It really started to come together when Amy told me about all her research into the history and varieties of grapes, plus their worth."

Phil's nodding. "Most people don't realize the money that's made from grapes. Sure, a few families stand out, but you don't have to be a winery to be wealthy."

"All the signs were pointing at a DiFazio link, but we didn't know who. The threats to the Bonhams for telling their story may have involved management who didn't want the public to know they were allowing a hooker to come to the labor camp. And management had to be involved if grapes were sold under fraudulent names." Dodson says.

"That's the thing that I wondered about." Clarice sets her cup down hard enough to slosh some coffee out, but catches it before it drips onto the summer blouse she's wearing. In fact, she looks suspiciously like she's put on a touch of makeup...definitely some mascara. "If it was a fiddle about the kind of grapes they were selling, why would the fieldworkers know?"

"Remember, Clar, quite a few of those workers, including *jefe*, were year-round employees. They'd know exactly what varieties were where. They even complained that the harvesting was scattered."

"That's the crux, Amy." Dodson takes the lead again. "When Felix was booked on murder charges, he was willing to talk...a lot. This fraud had been going on for several years. They'd harvest all the older varieties...carignan, Barbera, Pinot, and send them off to be crushed as red table wine. Some of them, though were put into gondolas, topped off with Zins and sent off as Zins. They never completely substituted another grape for a Zin, but they were selling mixed grapes. The field workers knew that, they knew the vines. The truck driver, Manual Oropeza, was in on it because he had to sign for the load, the winery workers who checked the load in were in on it."

"That's an awful lot of people who knew about this. I'm surprised someone didn't talk." I offer around the coffee pot.

"Someone did try to talk. The two field workers. They went to *jefe* and demanded higher wages because they knew about the fraud. And they told Oropeza what they were doing." Dodson is shaking his head.

Clarice looks perplexed. "Why Angel? She certainly didn't want any more money."

"No, she suffered from having too much knowledge. She talked to *jefe* about the murder victims and had to be shut up. They were some of her regulars, and she'd given them some heroin as a sort of thank you. Just a taste, because she never had enough to sell and knew they couldn't afford it anyway. Once *jefe* heard that, heroin was a perfect red herring."

I'm quiet. In fact, we are all silent for a moment. Three people dead, untold misery for a local family, all because grapes equaled money.

"That answers *jefe's* role. But he didn't put this together. He wasn't in a situation where he could just pocket the extra money." There are still some pieces missing.

"You're right, Amy. There was a DiFazio involved."

"Oh, lord did Carmine or Jules set this up? What a blow to the family!"

Dodson purses his lips. "No, it was Danny. He's Jules' nephew and the Chief Financial Officer. He's been embezzling and fudging the books for the last five years. Nobody checked because they were making money, and he's a family member. As long as everybody kept silent, there was enough money to go around."

I'm aghast. "You mean a family member hired, or ordered, a trusted employee, *jefe*, to murder people just to keep the scam quiet?"

"No." Dodson's shaking his head. "Felix took that on himself. He'd worked his way up to field supervisor, was able to bring his family from Mexico, had a regular house, and was on the road to citizenship. And two of his crew were blackmailing him to increase their payout. He talked it over with Danny who said they needed to be stopped. Who knows what Danny meant, but Felix stopped them the only way he knew how. Permanently."

Jorge Felix had planned this for weeks. When Angel came out to visit the camp, he made sure he "saw" her first. He offered to keep her purse occasionally while she was with the workers. He took one of her needles and twice stole small amounts of heroin. Since she never mentioned any missing needles or drugs, he felt safe.

He and Oropeza grabbed the first worker, Jesus, shot him full of heroin and then slit his throat and stabbed him, leaving his body tucked under the vines, heavy and ripe with large bunches. They used both a grape knife and a small machete, so it would look like he'd gotten in a fight with some other workers.

The second murder was easier. They had the routine down. Heroin first, then slicing and stabbing. Dodson said Felix told him they gave them heroin first, both to make sure the drug was circulating through their bodies and to partially knock them out.

"Angel was more difficult. She was used to the drug so Manual hit her with a tire iron before they dragged her down by the river and stabbed her." Dodson sighs. "I don't know if Danny had this in mind."

CHAPTER FORTY-SEVEN

CLARICE has been in court all morning. It's the arraignment of Jorge Felix on first-degree murder charges and Danny DiFazio on theft and solicitation of murder for hire.

This news hits Monroe like a sledgehammer. We run stories on Felix' arrest, Danny DiFazio's arrest, reaction from Carmine and Jules DiFazio—mostly "No comment"—everybody's lawyered up and what's left of the DiFazio empire is frantically harvesting grapes to salvage what they can.

Nobody's won in this debacle, even Skies and the DEA/FBI team. They had to settle for writing off the murders of Jackson Smythe and Ricky Bob Thomas as small-time casualties in the drug wars before they packed their bags and headed for better hunting grounds.

When she comes back from court, Clarice is subdued. She's an adrenaline junkie and getting the bad guys usually puts her on a high. This time, though, the story has a personal edge. She knew Angel. She knows the Bonhams. She's been threatened. There's not a lot of joy in these stories.

I ask if she wants to come over for a swim after work and she says, "Sure."

Mac greets her at the door, his whole body wiggling with

happiness. I say, "Want a glass of wine?"
"Do you have any iced tea? I think I'm off wine for a bit."
It's been a vintage harvest.

ACKNOWLEDGEMENTS

There are so many people who've helped me tell this story.

There are the women in my critique group; Pam Giarrizzo, June Gillam, Mertianna Georgia and Linda Townsdin who, as always, are invaluable. And yes, we drank a lot of wine along with suggestions, corrections, explanations and critiques.

There are the Grannies who tell stories and Illa and Don Collin, who answer my questions.

There are the beta readers; Angie Gleason, Jackie Timmons, Karolyn Simon, Kim VanDeusen and the always eagle-eyed Beth White.

And there are the "wine guys." Darrell Corti, the wine expert at Sacramento's Corti Brothers Market; and Axel Borg, Bibliographer in the Bio/Ag Department and John Sherlock, Rare Books Librarian at the Shields Library, University of California at Davis.

Finally, and most importantly, there are Darcy and Matt, and Mother and Idee. You are the past and the future and I love you.